NEVER WEAR

Red Lipstick

ON PICTURE DAY

(AND OTHER LESSONS I'VE LEARNED)

DON'T MISS MANDY BERR'S
EARLIER ADVENTURES!

DON'T WEAR

Polka-Dot Underwear

WITH WHITE PANTS
(AND OTHER LESSONS I'VE LEARNED)

* * *

A CAST IS THE

Perfect Accessory

(AND OTHER LESSONS I'VE LEARNED)

NEVER WEAR

Red Lipstick

ON PICTURE DAY
(AND OTHER LESSONS I'VE LEARNED)

BY ALLISON GUTKNECHT
ILLUSTRATED BY STEVIE LEWIS

ALADDIN
NEW YORK   LONDON   TORONTO   SYDNEY   NEW DELHI

This book is a work of fiction. Any references to historical events, real people, or real places are used fictitiously. Other names, characters, places, and events are products of the author's imagination, and any resemblance to actual events or places or persons, living or dead, is entirely coincidental.

ALADDIN

An imprint of Simon & Schuster Children's Publishing Division
1230 Avenue of the Americas, New York, NY 10020
First Aladdin paperback edition November 2014
Text copyright © 2014 by Allison Gutknecht
Illustrations copyright © 2014 by Stevie Lewis
Also available in an Aladdin hardcover edition.
All rights reserved, including the right of reproduction in whole or
in part in any form.
ALADDIN is a trademark of Simon & Schuster, Inc., and related logo is a
registered trademark of Simon & Schuster, Inc.
For information about special discounts for bulk purchases, please contact Simon &
Schuster Special Sales at 1-866-506-1949 or business@simonandschuster.com.
The Simon & Schuster Speakers Bureau can bring authors to your live event. For
more information or to book an event, contact the Simon & Schuster Speakers
Bureau at 1-866-248-3049 or visit our website at www.simonspeakers.com.
Cover designed by Jessica Handelman
The text of this book was set in Arno Pro.
The illustrations for this book were rendered digitally.
Manufactured in the United States of America 1014 OFF
2 4 6 8 10 9 7 5 3 1
Library of Congress Control Number 2014939256
ISBN 978-1-4814-2959-7 (hc)
ISBN 978-1-4814-2958-0 (pbk)
ISBN 978-1-4814-2960-3 (eBook)

For Cioci,
WHO KNEW THE IMPORTANCE OF
A STRICT BEAUTY REGIMEN

Many thanks to

ALYSON HELLER FOR NEVER FAILING IN THE SNAZZY IDEA
AND GLITTERY ENTHUSIASM DEPARTMENTS,
CHARLIE OLSEN FOR ALWAYS LOOKING OUT FOR MANDY AND ME,
AND SARAH JANE ABBOTT AND PAUL CRICHTON FOR THEIR
WORK IN SPREADING MANDY'S MESSAGES!

SPECIAL SHOUT-OUT TO
LEXIE CROSSLAND, WHO HAS THE BEST PICTURE DAY PHOTO
OF ALL TIME (AT LEAST MANDY AND I THINK SO!).

ENDLESS APPRECIATION TO
THE TEAMS AT ALADDIN AND INKWELL FOR HELPING TO
PERFECT THE POLKA DOTS.

Contents

CHAPTER 1

Fancy-Dancy Copycats

MRS. SPANGLE IS GETTING ON MY NERVES.

Sometimes Mrs. Spangle is the best second-grade teacher in the universe, and other times she is not. Today she is not, because we do not agree about when I should be allowed to wear my fancy-dancy sunglasses. Grandmom gave me these sunglasses, and they are just amazing, if I am being honest. Only, Mrs. Spangle does not think they are as amazing as I do, because when I put them on while I am doing my seatwork, I hear her clear her

throat, and she does not do so very quietly either. I look over at her through my sunglasses, and she is staring right at me.

"Mandy," she begins, "you know the rule about no sunglasses inside the school." She gestures for me to take them off and then looks down at her desktop.

I glance at the list of eight rules for our classroom, which hangs next to the board, then I shoot my hand in the air. When Mrs. Spangle does not call on me, I start to wave it, still wearing my sunglasses.

"Yes?" Mrs. Spangle finally sees me.

"There is no rule about sunglasses," I say quietly, pointing to the list. "So I will just wear these, okay?"

"Not okay," Mrs. Spangle says, and she begins rustling in her desk drawer. She pulls out a black marker, walks over to our CLASSROOM RULES sign, and takes the cap off. "Sorry to interrupt your work, boys and girls, but who can tell me some accessories we are not allowed to wear inside the school building?"

Hands shoot in the air all around me, but I just cross my arms and slouch down in my seat.

"Yes, Julia?" Mrs. Spangle calls.

"Hats," Julia answers.

"Right." Mrs. Spangle begins writing a new rule—number nine—on our list. "No hats. . . . What else? Natalie?"

"Sunglasses," Natalie answers, and I give her a dirty look, which is a waste because she cannot even see it through my sunglasses.

"Ahem." Mrs. Spangle clears her throat again at me, but I pretend not to hear her. She writes *sunglasses* next to *hats* on our new rule number nine. "What else?"

"Polka-dot underwear!" Dennis calls out super loudly, and I whip around in my seat real fast and stick my tongue out at him.

"No underwear talk in school, Dennis," Mrs. Spangle says. "I'll tell you what—I'm going to finish this rule with 'No hats, sunglasses, or other outdoor accessories can be worn in the classroom.'" She dots the new rule with a period, even though I think it would be better with an exclamation mark, and she turns to face me. Mrs. Spangle and I stare at each other in silence.

"Mandy, sunglasses off. Now," she finally says, so I pull the sunglasses off of my face and fold them on top of my desk.

"Inside your desk, please," Mrs. Spangle continues, and I don't know what she has against fancy-dancy sunglasses. "You can wear them when you're outside at recess, but not one minute before." I place my sunglasses inside my desk and cover them with a sheet of construction paper to protect them.

Anya leans over and whispers in my ear, "Sorry about your sunglasses," and this is why Anya is my favorite person in the world, at least most of the time. Because she understands what a tragedy it is to not be able to wear your fancy-dancy sunglasses during seatwork.

I nod my head sadly at her, and then I feel a tap on my elbow. I turn, and Natalie is holding out her hand in a fist toward me, real low so Mrs. Spangle cannot see.

"What is it?" I whisper-yell at her.

Natalie shakes her fist up and down. "Take it," she whispers.

I reach out my hand toward hers, and she drops a slip of paper in my palm. I open it carefully so that it doesn't make any crinkling sounds. *I have a surprise to show you at recess,* I read.

I turn to her. "What is it?" I ask.

"It's a surprise," Natalie says.

"I would like to know now."

"Mandy!" Mrs. Spangle yells from across the room. "Meet me at my desk, please." I stand up slowly and walk across the classroom with my head down.

"Ooh, Polka Dot's in trouble," Dennis whispers from behind me, but I do not say anything back because I do not want Mrs. Spangle to yell my name again. Even if she is getting on my nerves right now, I still want her to like me more than she likes Dennis.

Mrs. Spangle sits in her chair when we both reach her desk so that she can look straight into my eyes. "What's going on with you today?"

I shrug my shoulders because I do not know how to answer that.

"I'd like a reason for why you're being so difficult."

I look down at my shoes sadly and wiggle

my toes inside of them. "I just really like my sunglasses," I tell her softly. I look up quickly to see Mrs. Spangle's face, and she is smiling at me then, just a little bit. So she cannot be too angry with me if she is smiling.

"You know, I like my sunglasses, too," Mrs. Spangle tells me. "But that still doesn't mean I wear them inside the school. Got it?"

I nod my head, because I think I am almost done being in trouble.

"But more importantly, when I ask you to do something, I need you to follow directions," Mrs. Spangle continues. "The first time."

"Okay, I will try," I say, because that is the truth.

"I hope so," Mrs. Spangle says. "You were being very ornery just now."

"What's that?" I ask her.

"Ornery? It means you're being hard to get along with," Mrs. Spangle explains.

"Like a crankypants?"

"Something like that." Mrs. Spangle smiles at me again, and she reaches out her hand toward mine. "So do we have a deal? No more ornery behavior?"

"Deal!" I reach out my hand and shake hers firmly.

"Good. Now get back to your seatwork, please—the faster you get your work done, the sooner recess will seem to get here. And you know what that means?"

"Fancy-dancy sunglasses time," I answer. "Wahoo!"

"Now get to it." Mrs. Spangle points me back toward my desk, and I trot away and finish my seatwork in a lick and a split.

Natalie's note is still resting on top of my desk, so I flip it over and write on the other side: *What is the surprise?* I glance at Mrs. Spangle's desk to see if she is watching me, and I wonder if passing this note back to Natalie is something that she will consider "ornery." I think as long as I am quiet about it, I will be okay, so when I am sure Mrs. Spangle isn't watching, I reach over and tap Natalie on the elbow before dropping the paper in her lap. I watch Natalie read the note out of the corner of my eye, and in teeny-tiny letters, she writes one back to me. She drops the paper on the floor in between our chairs, and I reach down to grab it, again without making one sound.

You will love it, Natalie has written, but I am not sure how Natalie is so certain that she knows what I love. She is not Anya, after all.

"What is the surprise?" I ask Natalie the second the lunch aides open the doors leading to the playground. I pull my fancy-dancy sunglasses out of my lunch box and stick them on my nose, even though the sun is hiding behind the clouds.

"I'll show you on the swings," Natalie tells me, and she is grinning like she has a special secret.

"Do you know?" I ask Anya.

"Nope," Anya answers, and she begins to skip ahead of us.

"Oh, come on," I say to Natalie. "Stop holding your horses."

"Okay," Natalie answers, and she reaches into the pocket of her jacket. Slowly, she pulls out her hand and uncurls her fingers, revealing what she is holding.

"Aren't they great?" Natalie asks. "Now I have my own pair of fancy-dancy sunglasses too!"

And this is just about the furthest thing from great news that I have ever heard in my life.

"Do you like them?" Natalie asks, putting them on her face. And they look kind of silly, to tell you the truth, because Natalie has to wear her sunglasses *over* her regular glasses, and that is not how fancy-dancy sunglasses are supposed to look. But her sunglasses are . . . well, they are glittery, and they are purple, which is almost periwinkle, and they sort of make Natalie look like a cat.

And I *love* them. Even more than I love my own fancy-dancy sunglasses.

And this makes me feel a little bit angry, because I liked my glasses the best before I saw how beautiful Natalie's are.

Anya turns around and says. "I love them. I think they're great."

This comment makes Natalie grin wider than a jack-o'-lantern, and I scowl at Anya.

"Mandy? Don't you like them?" Natalie asks me.

"I like *my* sunglasses," I tell Natalie, because that is the truth. I run ahead of both Anya and

Natalie and grab a swing on the far end of the set, one where neither of them can sit next to me.

"Hey, you didn't save me a swing." Anya runs up beside me.

"Do you like Natalie's sunglasses better than mine?" I ask her.

"I like them both," Anya tells me, which is not a great answer.

"But I had mine first," I say. "Natalie copycatted me."

"You still like yours, don't you?" Anya asks.

"Yes." I pause. "But I think I might like Natalie's better now. And that makes me mad."

"Don't be mad about it," Anya says. "I'm going to play on the monkey bars since you didn't save me a swing."

"Fine," I call after her, and I push on the ground with my toes so I can swing myself high in the air, just me and my sunglasses flying through the sky.

* * *

"Remember, hats, sunglasses, and other outdoor accessories off," Mrs. Spangle reminds us as we walk back into our classroom after recess. But I am already holding my sunglasses in my hand, because they do not seem nearly as fancy-dancy anymore.

"You're not mad at me, are you?" Anya scoots up behind me by the cubbies.

"No," I answer, because I do not really feel like being mad at Anya anyway.

But I might still feel like being mad at Natalie.

"Take your seats quickly so I can hand out your Picture Day reminders," Mrs. Spangle calls to us. "Remember to tell your parents that if they haven't submitted your order forms yet, we need them by next Wednesday."

"Wahoo!" I call as I return to my seat. "I love Picture Day."

"I hate Picture Day," Dennis calls out, because Dennis is terrible. "You should hate it too, Polka Dot. No one wants a picture of your face." He says this part in a whisper as he passes me.

"Quiet, Freckle Face," I answer just as softly, so that Mrs. Spangle cannot hear. "The camera probably can't even see your face through all the freckles."

"Paper Passers, please come up to my desk to help me hand out the sheets," Mrs. Spangle says. "Remember, class: Next Wednesday come dressed in your best Picture Day outfits. We all want to look nice for our class photo."

"So don't wear your polka-dot underwear, Polka Dot," Dennis whispers to me again, and I see Anya kick him under their desks.

I decide then that I am going to come up with the best, fanciest-danciest Picture Day accessory in the whole world, and I am not going to make one peep about it to Natalie beforehand, or else she might try to copy it.

And then I will give one of my largest Picture Day photos to Mrs. Spangle to keep on her desk, and I will sign the back of it, *To the best second-grade teacher in the universe. Love, Mandy*— just to remind her that she should always like me more than she likes Dennis.

Even when we do get on each other's nerves.

CHAPTER 2

The Handbag Caper

"I NEED A NEW ACCESSORY!" I YELL as I bang through the front door after school.

"Mandy, I thought we talked about not letting that door slam," Mom answers me. "We can't have special you-and-me time without the twins if you wake them up." And I do not think they should have to hear so much, but I still place my book bag on the couch without a sound, because I definitely do not want to hear the twins' howls right now.

"I need a new accessory," I repeat more quietly. "It is very important."

"What do you mean?"

"Yeah, what do you mean?" Timmy calls up from the floor, and I do not know why he thinks a three-year-old should be part of a grown-up conversation about accessories.

"I cannot wear my fancy-dancy sunglasses anymore," I state.

"Why not?" Mom asks. "I thought they were your favorite thing ever?"

"Yeah, why not?" Timmy repeats.

"STOP BEING A COPYCAT!" I yell at him. "*That* is why I cannot wear my sunglasses anymore. Because Natalie is a copycat too."

"Natalie got her own pair of sunglasses?" Mom guesses, and she is a much better listener about my problems when the twins are not around, I think.

"Yes, and she has to wear them over her own glasses, which is not how fancy-dancy sunglasses work," I tell her.

"You know what they say, Mandy," Mom begins, "imitation is the greatest form of flattery. Natalie got sunglasses too because she thought you looked so nice in them."

I shake my head back and forth ferociously. "Fancy-dancy sunglasses were *my* accessory, and now Natalie stole them. It's not fair."

"You know what kind of attitude that sounds like to me?" Mom asks as she plops down on the couch. "B-R-A-T."

"Brat!" Timmy calls out, and I stomp my foot in his direction.

"Didn't we fix that B-R-A-T behavior after the whole broken-toe incident? No backtracking, please," Mom says. "Eight years old is too old to act that way."

"But this is an *emergency*," I explain, because "emergency" is the kind of word that gets grown-ups to listen to you. "Picture Day is next week, and I need a new fancy-dancy accessory for my picture."

"You can't wear sunglasses on Picture Day anyway," Mom says. "Besides, you already have your periwinkle dress from the Presidential Pageant. I think that will make a perfect Picture Day outfit."

"But I wore that already," I remind her. "Everybody saw that dress, so now it is boring. And Natalie could copycat it."

"I'm sure Natalie is not going to wear the same dress as you on Picture Day," Mom says. "With all the outfits out there in the world, I am positive she'll choose something different."

"I am not positive," I answer. "Plus, a dress is not even an accessory. I need an accessory."

"You have plenty of accessories in your room," Mom says. "Why don't you try one of them out for a while? Your pastel bangle bracelets or your Rainbow Sparkle headband or—"

"I've worn all of those already," I repeat, and Mom sighs an enormous breath at me.

"I don't know what to tell you, Mandy," she replies. "I'm not buying you anything new, so if this accessory business is so important to you, you better problem-solve with what you already have." I scrunch my lips over to one side of my mouth into a pout. "Now, Timmy has been waiting all day for someone to play hide-and-seek with him, and I think it would be really nice if—"

"No, thank you," I say, and I turn around quickly and head up the stairs before Mom can make me play with a preschooler.

"Remember," Mom calls after me, "your dad and I are going to that dinner tonight, so

Grandmom is babysitting." I smile at this news when I reach the top of the stairs, because I no longer need Mom to help me get a new accessory for Picture Day.

I will just ask Grandmom for one instead.

"Anybody home?" Grandmom calls when she arrives at our house at dinnertime. Timmy bounds down the stairs loudly to greet her and throws his arms around her knees. "Give me some sugar," she says to him, and Timmy plants a kiss on her lips.

When I get to the bottom of the stairs, I look around to make sure Mom is not there snooping.

"How's my favorite fancy-schmancy girl?" Grandmom reaches out to hug me, and I hold on to her tightly so that my mouth is close to her ear.

"I need to tell you something," I whisper.

"Mandy was a brat," Timmy tattletales, but I

ignore him because I do not have much time.

"I need something to wear for Picture Day, please," I whisper to Grandmom, and I think I spit on her a little bit.

"Ooh, sounds fun," Grandmom says. "I'll help you pick something out tonight. Is tomorrow Picture Day?"

"No, next week," I say. "And I need something *new* for Picture Day. This is very important."

"Why is it so important?" Grandmom asks as Timmy tries to scramble up her legs until she picks him up. "You already have plenty of lovely clothes in your closet."

"Everybody has seen them already," I explain. "And there are many copycats in my class—well, mostly Natalie—so if I do not wear something brand new, she might wear the same thing. And that would be a tragedy."

"Oh, good, you're here," Mom says, coming

into the living room, all dressed up in high heels and everything. "The twins are already down for the night, so hopefully, you won't hear much out of them. There's some leftover baked chicken in the refrigerator for these two—"

"Yuck," I interrupt her.

"You love chicken," Mom says to me.

"I hate leftovers," I explain, but Mom begins to smear lipstick across her lips instead of answering me.

"Can I have some?" I ask.

"Lipstick?" Mom grabs me by the chin and plants a wet kiss on my lips. "There, now you're wearing some too," she says, even though that was not what I had in mind. "Tim, are you ready?"

"Coming." Dad walks into the room and says good-bye to each of us quickly before they both run out the door.

"So about Picture Day . . . ," I begin again in my sweetest voice.

"If you're trying to get me to buy you new clothes, that's not going to work," Grandmom tells me. "Especially after I just got you those sunglasses."

"But I cannot even wear them anymore because Natalie copycatted—"

"I know, I know, Natalie's a copycat. I think it's time you and Natalie worked out your differences once and for all, don't you?" Grandmom asks, walking toward the kitchen with Timmy trailing behind her.

The front door flies open then, and Mom comes back into the living room. "Forgot my handbag," she says, and she reaches toward the couch for a small bag, which is the color of a snake. She places her lipstick tube inside and heads back out again. "Love you!" she calls to me over her shoulder, and her snake bag is the last thing I see before she closes the door.

"Come on, Mandy, let's have some dinner," Grandmom calls from the kitchen.

And I don't even mind so much anymore that dinner is leftovers. Because Mom has just given me a great idea for my new accessory, one that is lying on the floor of my closet. So maybe, just maybe, leftover things are not as bad as I thought.

The next morning I place my fancy-dancy sunglasses on my nightstand sadly, because I do not feel like bringing them to school anymore. Instead, I grab the pink handbag that my cousin, Paige, mailed to me for my birthday. I usually hate pink, and I don't love handbags, either, but if Mom takes her snake bag out for special occasions, I guess handbags are a pretty grown-up accessory. Plus, this handbag has fringe on

the side, and it feels almost like feathers when I pet it. And there are many gemstones lining the top of the fringe, and I do love shiny things.

The problem with this handbag, though, is that I do not have anything fun to put inside of it, like lipstick or gum. I walk around my room, and I try to push my stuffed Rainbow Sparkle inside, but she is too big. And then I place my three swirly marbles in it, but they clang together when I walk, so Mrs. Spangle might hear them and take them away.

"Mandy, let's go!" Mom calls from downstairs. "Your cereal is getting soggy." I reach under my pillow and grab a handful of gummy bears, and I pour them inside my handbag.

The reason I do not love handbags is that it is very, very easy to forget about them. You can put your sunglasses on top of your head and— ta-da!—they are right there, but you always have to think about where your handbag is. I already have to worry about my book bag and my lunch box and now this bag, too—it is very tiring.

When I get to school, I put my handbag in my cubby, because I do not know if Mrs. Spangle thinks it is an outdoor accessory or not. When Mrs. Spangle calls my group to line up for lunch, I place the strap of my bag over my shoulder and run my fingers through the fringe. It is not so bad for a handbag, I guess—it is pretty fancy-dancy, after all, even if it is pink.

I plop my handbag on the cafeteria table next to my lunch box, and the gemstones click against the top of the table.

"Pretty bag," Anya says to me.

"Yeah," Natalie agrees.

"Thank you," I answer proudly. "My cousin, Paige, gave it to me."

"I think I have one just like it," Natalie tells

me, and my eyes grow wide like pancakes then, because there is no way I am going to let Natalie copycat my handbag, too.

"You cannot bring it to school," I tell her. "You already stole my fancy-dancy sunglasses."

"What are you talking about? I didn't steal your sunglasses," Natalie says. "I got my own pair."

"That is pretty much the same thing," I say. "Because now I cannot wear mine anymore."

"Yes, you can," Natalie says. "I think it would be fun. Anya could get some too, and then we could be triplets."

"Twins are not fun, so triplets are even worse," I say, opening my lunch box. "Oh, blech." The inside of my box is soggy from a leak in my sandwich bag. There is mayonnaise all over my napkin, and the whole thing feels like a damp twin.

"Anya, help me," I say, picking up the napkin carefully between two fingers while Anya wipes up the rest of the mayonnaise with her own napkin. We bring them to the trash can in the middle of the cafeteria.

And when we get back, my handbag is gone.

"Hey!" I yell. "Who took my handbag?" I look straight into Natalie's eyes, but she only shrugs, ignoring me. "Did you take it?"

"No."

"Then who did?"

Natalie shrugs again.

"Natalie!" I slam my palms against the top of the cafeteria table, and it kind of hurts a lot. But that's when I hear it from over my shoulder: words coming from the most terrible, horrible voice.

"Mmm," the voice begins, "gummy bears!"

I turn and see Dennis placing an entire

handful of gummy bears—*my* gummy bears—into his mouth. I feel my insides bubble up until they come out of my mouth in the loudest, screechiest, most piercing scream I have ever created.

And I am pretty impressed with the scream, if I am being honest.

But the lunch aides are not, because they all come barreling over to where I am standing. Natalie has her hands covering her ears, as if I might start screaming again at any moment.

"What happened over here? Who's hurt?" They talk over one another, all looking at me because I am the only one still standing.

"He stole my handbag!" I explain, pointing at the boys' cafeteria table.

"Take a seat, young lady," the lunch aide with the kittens on her sweatshirt yells at me, and I do not think it is right for someone who wears cats that look so friendly on her shirt to sound so mean. "You had no reason to scream like that over something so silly."

"But—but—" I cannot even get my words out because I am so upset. "He stole my handbag, and he *ate* my *gummy bears!*"

"Who?"

"HIM!" I turn around and point right at Dennis.

"Come with me, young man." The lunch aide waves her finger at him. "What is your name?"

"Dennis!" I answer for him. "Dennis Riley!"

"That's enough from you, thank you," the lunch aide scolds me. "Mr. Riley, I assume that handbag isn't yours. Please return it." Dennis throws the bag in my lap without saying a word as the aide leads him out of the cafeteria.

"He should be very, very punished!" I yell after them. "And never touch my things again, Freckle Face!" I slap my empty handbag down on the cafeteria table and glare at Natalie.

"I know you saw him take it," I say, and Natalie shrugs again.

"Maybe you shouldn't have been so mean about the sunglasses," she replies. And with that, I take the entire rest of my lunch and dump it all into the trash can in the middle of the cafeteria.

Because Dennis and Natalie have made me lose my appetite.

CHAPTER 3

Wahoo Girl

DENNIS IS BACK IN OUR CLASSROOM after lunch, which I do not think should be allowed, because Dennis shouldn't be able to come to school again for the entire rest of the year. Maybe not even until we go to middle school. Or maybe he should just move.

"What are *you* doing here?" I ask as I walk to my seat, and for once, Dennis keeps his big mouth shut. He is sitting with his hands folded on top of his desk, and he does not even look up at me.

And Dennis looks pretty sad, actually, which kind of makes me happy.

"What's the matter, Dennis?" Anya teases him. "Cat got your tongue?" But Dennis doesn't answer her, either.

"Take your seats, everyone," Mrs. Spangle calls. "Mr. Jacks will be in to talk to all of you in a few minutes."

I feel my face get hot then, and I snap my head around to look at Anya. She looks back at me with jumpiness in her eyes, because having the principal come to your classroom is *never* a good sign. It is a terrible sign, really.

I glance over at Natalie, and she looks much more terrified than Anya and I do, because I don't think Natalie has ever seen Principal Jacks in her life. Even at school assemblies, she probably looks away. Because the principal means trouble, and Natalie is allergic to trouble.

I have met Principal Jacks face-to-face only one time, and it was by mistake. On the first day of school in kindergarten, my teacher sent me to the office with the attendance sheet, and I got a little bit lost. Well, I found the office, but I did not stop at the secretary's desk like I was supposed to. Instead, I walked straight back into Principal Jacks's office, and there he was, sitting at his desk, staring at me.

Principal Jacks kind of looks like an owl, if I am being honest. He has round glasses and no hair on his head, except for some tufts on the sides that look like feathers. And owls can be pretty scary when you see them up close. So when I accidentally went into his office, I froze on my own two feet, and I could not make them move forward or backward. I just stared at Principal Jacks and thought about how he looked like an owl.

Finally, Principal Jacks said, "Mrs. Gradey, looks like we have a trespasser," and the secretary came to fetch me. He was not very mean about it, so that is something, but that does not mean that I am any less scared of him today. This is why, when he walks into Mrs. Spangle's classroom, I am almost as nervous to see him as Natalie seems to be.

"Good afternoon." Principal Jacks stares down at us through his round owl glasses. No one says a word.

"Good afternoon," Principal Jacks repeats.

"Good afternoon," my class mumbles back to him.

"I hear we had some more excitement in the cafeteria today," he says, and I turn to look at Dennis. Dennis's ears turn bright red at the tips, and he does not look up from his desktop.

"This isn't the first incident of this kind,

unfortunately, and frankly, I've had enough of this lack of decorum in the cafeteria. The students of Roselee Elementary School are better than that. Am I right?"

My class and I all nod our heads.

"In order to help us work on our behavior, we've been planning a little cafeteria contest for you all, which I've decided to put into place sooner rather than later," Principal Jacks tells us. And before I can think better of it, I hear a "Wahoo!" escape from my mouth, because I love a contest. But then I throw my hands over my lips, because I can't believe I just "wahooed" at the principal. I look over at Mrs. Spangle, and she has her face bent down toward the floor, her shoulders shaking.

"You like the sound of that?" I hear Principal Jacks ask, but I keep looking at Mrs. Spangle, trying to figure out why her shoulders are trembling up and down.

"Excuse me," Principal Jacks says, and he snaps his fingers. And I have always wanted to learn to snap, so I stare at his hand and try to figure out how he did it.

"Mandy," I hear Mrs. Spangle's voice say. "Mr. Jacks is talking to you," and I take my eyes away from Principal Jacks's hand and look back at Mrs. Spangle. I can tell then by the smile that is still stuck in the corners of her mouth why her shoulders were shaking after my "Wahoo!": she was laughing! And I love to make Mrs. Spangle laugh.

I turn back to Principal Jacks, and my stomach suddenly feels shaky from nervousness.

"You like the sound of the contest?" Principal Jacks asks. "I didn't even tell you what it's for yet."

"I just really like contests," I answer quietly.

"What do you like about them?" Principal Jacks asks, and his owl eyes seem to be grinning at me.

"I like winning them," I answer honestly, and

now it is Principal Jacks's turn to laugh at me. But he is not laughing at me in a mean way—he is laughing like he thinks I am funny.

And I kind of really like Principal Jacks right then.

"Well, I hope you'll want to win this one after you hear what the prize is," Principal Jacks continues. "Each day the lunch aides are going to be handing out raffle tickets to those students who they feel are doing the best jobs of being courteous, well behaved, and mannerly in the cafeteria. Every time you get a ticket, you can write your name on it and stick it in the giant jar that Mrs. Gradey is going to place outside of the office. To get the ball rolling, we're going to hold our first drawing on Wednesday afternoon, which is what special day around here?"

My classmates shoot their hands in the air, but no one shoots it as high as me.

"Yes, you again," Principal Jacks calls on me. "Boy, we have an eager beaver in this one, don't we, Mrs. Spangle?"

And I am not sure why Principal Jacks is calling me a beaver, but I do know that next Wednesday is Picture Day, which is practically the best day of the year. "Picture Day!" I blurt out, and then I follow that up with another "Wahoo," just to see if it will make him laugh again or, even better, snap his fingers.

"Right," Principal Jacks says, and he chuckles. "Our first drawing will be on Picture Day, and the chosen winner each week will get to have lunch with me. But remember, you can't win without a raffle ticket, and you can't get a raffle ticket without perfect behavior in the cafeteria. The better your behavior every day, the better your chances of winning. Understood?"

We nod our heads up and down.

"Oh, and I forgot to mention: These lunches

are going to take place in the Teachers' Lounge on Fridays. We'll do it as many times as we need to in order to make the Roselee Elementary School students the best-behaved cafeteria-goers in the entire nation. How does that sound to you—what is your name again?"

Principal Jacks is looking right at me.

"Me?" I point to my chest.

"Yes, the 'Wahoo Girl,'" Principal Jacks answers, and I am pretty happy that Dennis is so down in the dumps right now, because if he were not, I am almost positive he would give me the new namecall of "Wahoo Girl."

"Mandy," I answer him. "Mandy Berr."

"Well, how does that contest sound to you, Mandy Berr?"

"Excellent," I answer. "I would like to win it." And that is the truth, because not only do I like to win things, but I would definitely like to have lunch with Principal Jacks, since he thinks I am funny. Plus, the lunch is in the Teachers' Lounge, and I have always wanted to see inside of there, because students are not usually allowed. And I think it is probably a very interesting place, with vending machines and everything.

"Great," Principal Jacks says. "I hope you all feel the same and will be on your best behavior in the cafeteria this week and, well, every week. And I hope we never have to have this kind of conversation again." And I am not positive, but I am pretty sure that he's looking in Dennis's direction right then.

But Dennis still does not look up from his desk, and even his Mohawk is starting to look droopy.

And I am sort of glad that he is acting so unhappy, because that is what happens when you steal handbags and gummy bears. Especially when they belong to me.

CHAPTER 4

Raffle Losers

"I AM GOING TO HAVE LUNCH with the principal," I announce to Mom in the kitchen after school.

"Ooooh," I hear Timmy's voice answer, but I do not see him anywhere.

"Oh yeah? Sounds exciting. How did that happen?" Mom asks.

"He is having a contest for us to win a lunch with him. Whoever has the best behavior in the cafeteria gets a raffle ticket."

"What's a raffle?" Timmy's voice interrupts again.

"WHERE ARE YOU?" I yell. "You are annoying me."

"Hide-and-seek!" Timmy calls back.

"You cannot play hide-and-seek and then talk from your hiding spot," I say. "That makes no sense." Although, if I am being honest, I am kind of impressed with wherever Timmy's hiding spot is, because I still do not see him anywhere. I peer underneath the table, behind the counter, and around the curtains, all very quickly so that Mom cannot tell I am looking for him. Because I try to never, ever play games with Timmy. He is a preschooler, and I am a second grader, and that would just be humiliating.

Plus, Timmy is gross.

"Find me!" Timmy's voice calls out again, and that's when I spot the piles of Tupperware stacked up on the kitchen floor, outside of the cabinet where Mom usually keeps them. I whip the door open and find Timmy crouched inside, smashed down like a turtle that has rolled onto its back.

"Get out of there, dummy," I say. "And start minding your own beeswax. I am having a conversation." I say "conversation" very seriously, because it is a word that grown-ups say this way when they do not want you to play your toy harmonica while they are on the phone.

"Mandy," Mom says with a warning in her voice. "What am I going to say?"

"Congratulations on having lunch with Principal Jacks?" I guess, even though I know that is not the right answer.

"No 'dummy' talk in this house. I'm tired of telling you these things," she says. "And did you actually win the contest yet?"

"No, it hasn't started," I answer. "Principal Jacks just announced it today."

"Well, that sounds fun," Mom says. "You

have good behavior in the cafeteria, don't you?"

"Usually," I answer, because that is the truth.

"What do you mean, usually?"

"Sometimes things happen," I explain. "In the cafeteria."

"What sorts of things?" Mom narrows her eyes at me.

"Like Dennis stealing my handbag."

Mom pauses. "What handbag?"

"The one Paige gave me."

"What was your handbag doing in school?"

"I needed it," I explain. "I told you—Natalie copycatted my fancy-dancy sunglasses, so I needed a new accessory, but then Dennis stole it and ate all of my gummy bears—"

"You brought gummy bears to school?" Mom interrupts me.

"That is not important," I say. "He stole my bag and ate my gummy bears and—"

"I've told you over and over that you can't eat gummy bears for lunch," Mom interrupts me again. "They are a special treat for when you're home and for when Dad and I say so. They're not for school."

I stop talking then, because Mom does not know about the bag of gummy bears from Grandmom that I still keep underneath my pillow, and it is best to keep it that way.

"So then what happened?" Mom asks. "After Dennis took the handbag that you shouldn't have had in school."

I think about how to answer this, because I know Mom is not going to like it no matter what. "I screamed," I finally tell her honestly.

"You screamed in school?"

"Yes," I say. "That is what girls do on TV whenever someone steals their handbag."

"Oh my goodness." Mom rubs her eyes with

her fingers, and she suddenly looks like she is ready to fall asleep. "None of this would have happened if you hadn't taken your handbag to school in the first place. This is not all Dennis's fault, you know."

I think about this for a moment. "But you take your handbag everywhere. Why can't I?"

"Because you are eight, Mandy. What do you possibly have to keep in your handbag? Besides, you have a book bag—you don't need both." And I guess grown-ups do not understand the importance of accessories like I do.

"I am done with this conversation now," I state, just like Mom and Dad do when they decide they don't want to be good listeners about my problems. I turn around and start to walk toward the stairs.

"Wait just a minute!" Mom calls after me. "You don't get to decide when conversations end—I do. Plus, you and Timmy have to get in that toy room and clean up the mess you made last week-end. I'm tired of stepping on LEGOs. I've been waiting all week."

"I was not playing with LEGOs," I say. "That was Timmy."

"You were playing with plenty else in there," Mom replies. "Let's go, you two. Get in there and work for the next twenty minutes. I'll set the timer. Timmy, out of the cabinet, please. Hide-and-seek is over."

I groan like a dinosaur and stomp my feet into the toy room. The place is covered in LEGOs and dolls and Matchbox cars and dress-up clothes and plastic animals and pretend food and . . . well, it is a pretty big mess. But most of this mess is Timmy's, so if I have to clean it up for him, then there is only one thing to do.

I am going to play hide-and-seek with his toys.

* * *

The next day at school Anya and I reach our cafeteria table, and Anya slams her lunch box down on top of it like we usually do. But instead of doing the same, I place my lunch box down quietly next to hers, sit on the bench, and open my box very carefully. Without saying a word, I remove my napkin, spread it out so that the four little squares turn into one giant tablecloth, and I place my sandwich bag on top. I then fold my hands in front of me and place them on the table, waiting.

"What is wrong with you?" Anya stares at me.

"I'm waiting until everyone else has their food ready before I start eating," I explain very softly. "It is the polite thing to do."

"But why?"

"Don't you remember? Principal Jacks's contest?" I remind her. "Whoever is the best behaved in the cafeteria is going to win a lunch with him. And I absolutely want to win."

"Why do you even want to?" Anya asks. "I would never want to have lunch with the principal." She makes a face like something stinks, and this is one reason why Anya is only my favorite person in the world *most* of the time and not *all* of the time—because she doesn't understand why having lunch with Principal Jacks would be the best thing ever.

"Didn't you hear that the lunch is in the Teachers' Lounge?" I ask. "I have always wanted to see inside that place. I think they have vending machines."

"I guess so," Anya answers. "But I'd rather have lunch with Mrs. Spangle than Mr. Jacks."

"Me too," I agree. "Except that Principal Jacks does know how to snap."

"Snap?"

"Yes, with his fingers," I explain. "Do you know how too?"

"Yeah," Anya answers, and she lifts up both hands, rubs her fingers together, and creates a loud popping sound. "Why?"

"Teach me, teach me," I say. "I have always wanted to know how."

But before Anya can show me one move, something hits me right in the middle of my back. "Yow!" I call out, and I turn around to see Dennis walking over to his table.

"Whoops," he calls back. "Sorry, Polka Dot. My elbow didn't see you there."

"YES, YOU DID!" I yell. "You did that on purpose."

"Folks in Mrs. Spangle's class," one of the lunch aides speaks into her megaphone. It is the same lady who was wearing the sweatshirt with the kittens on it yesterday, but now her shirt is covered in dogs. And cats are a much better animal to have on a shirt, if you ask me.

She walks over to our tables, dropping the megaphone to her side. "You two"—she points to Dennis and me—"I don't want to hear another peep out of either one of you. Got it?"

"But Dennis—"

"Nope!" the lunch aide says. "Remember Principal Jacks's contest. You two are definitely out of the raffle distribution for today. Let's not make it any worse than it already is." She turns away from our table and walks to the center of the cafeteria. So I lift up my lunch box and slam it back on the table. I dump all of the rest of my lunch out in front of me, crinkling my perfect napkin tablecloth and everything. And I do not even care now if I get crumbs on the table and jelly on the bench and juice on the floor, because I'm not getting a raffle ticket today anyway, so I will probably never get to see those vending machines.

CHAPTER 5

Makeup Makeover

MOM IS SITTING ON THE COUCH with her arms folded when I get home from school, and Timmy is right next to her mimicking the move. The twins are on a blanket in the middle of the living room, dumb baby toys all around them, which is just ridiculous because they are lying there like globs instead of playing with them.

"Why are the twins awake?" I ask, dumping my book bag and lunch box next to the front door. "They are supposed to be in bed so we can have special you-and-me time."

"Maybe you should spend more time worrying about what you're doing rather than the twins," Mom says. "Or Timmy, for that matter. Perhaps you'd care to explain what happened to all of the things you were supposed to clean up in the toy room?"

I glance at Timmy, and he is giving me his best dirty look, but he is not very good at making the face—mostly, he is just squinting his eyes closed. And everyone knows that the best way to give a dirty look is to glare with your eyes open.

"We're waiting, Mandy," Mom says. "Fess up."

"If you know already, then why are you asking me?" I say.

"I want to hear it from your own mouth," Mom says. "What did you do with the toys I told you to clean up?"

"Those were not my toys," I explain. "They were Timmy's. So I put them in his room."

Actually, I put them in Timmy's closet, in one giant pile on top of all of his shoes, but I do not include that detail.

"LEGOs in my sneaker!" Timmy cries out then. "It hurt my toes."

"You're the one who keeps wanting me to play hide-and-seek," I tell him. "I was hiding them for you."

"Nice try," Mom begins. "I think the words you're looking for are 'Sorry, Timmy.'"

I do not say anything at first, because I do not like apologizing to a preschooler for cleaning up his toys. Even if I did not put them in the right spot, he should thank me for helping him at all.

"I'll wait," Mom says. "The longer you take, the longer it will be before you get started putting all of the things you dumped in Timmy's closet back in the toy room—in the correct bins this time. And if you don't finish, well, guess what? There's a new episode of *Rainbow Sparkle* on TV tonight, isn't there? And I know who won't be watching it."

I scrunch up my lips and clench my hands into fists, because I absolutely, positively hate when Mom takes away Rainbow Sparkle's TV show as punishment, because she knows it is my favorite show ever.

"Sorry," I say slowly, but I keep my top and bottom teeth locked together so that it comes out as a hiss.

"Sorry who?"

"Sorry, Timmy," I finish.

"That's better," Mom says. "Now scoot upstairs and start bringing everything you dumped up there back to the toy room. And organize it so all the toys are in the right places this time, or else you're going to have to start over."

I turn on my heel and march up the stairs. When I reach the top, I walk into Timmy's room, which is a place I try never to go. The wallpaper is dark blue with planets all over it, and his bedspread is covered with dinosaurs, which does not even make sense because dinosaurs do not live in outer space. His room is much smaller than mine, so when he gets out of bed, he almost steps into his closet. His closet doors are wide open now, and all of the toys that I dumped inside are spilling out onto the floor.

I bend down and try to scoop up a big handful, but half of the LEGOs fall out of my hands before I can even stand. At this rate, it is going to take me all night to clean up Timmy's mess. I am going to need to find a big container to dump all of the toys in first. Yesterday I used two sand buckets, but they are still in the toy room, and I do not want to go all the way downstairs and pass Mom, Timmy, and the twins again in order to fetch them. Instead, I walk out of Timmy's room and into Mom and Dad's. I know Mom keeps a giant basket in their bathroom for dirty towels— that will be perfect for moving Timmy's toys.

I walk past their bed and into their bathroom, and I do not think it is fair that they get one in their room and I have to share the hallway bathroom with Timmy. I told Mom once that I would share her bathroom with her and Dad could share with Timmy, but Dad said, "Absolutely not" (though Mom seemed to think this was a pretty funny idea).

I tiptoe into their bathroom and stare at myself in the gigantic mirror above the sink. The mirror in my bathroom is big enough to see just my face, and that is only if I stand on a step stool, so I like this mirror much, much better. I take my hair down from its ponytail and lift Mom's round brush from the counter. I run the brush through my hair over and over, and it is pretty tangly at first, if I am being honest. But I count my brush-strokes until I reach fifty, which is how many times Rainbow Sparkle likes to be petted on her show. My hair looks very shiny then, and I open the middle drawer in between the sinks to see what else I can find.

I take out a bottle of Mom's favorite lotion and squirt a gigantic glob onto my hand. I run it back and forth in between my fingers, just like I see Mom do, but there is so much of it that I have to rub it on my face and my neck and my feet, too.

I dig farther into the drawer until I find it: Mom's makeup bag. Mom says I am allowed to wear makeup only on Halloween, but she gets to wear it much more than that, which I don't think is fair. I dig through the bag and find a container of pink blush, which I spread onto my cheeks and forehead and chin with a large, ticklish brush. Then I find the black mascara, and I remove the wand from the tube and try to place the stuff on my eyelashes very carefully, opening my eyes wide in the mirror so I can see better. The mascara ends up all around the outsides of my eyes, but the black dashes look like Rainbow Sparkle's whiskers, so I still like them.

At the bottom of the bag I find my very favorite type of makeup ever: lipstick! There are four tubes of lipstick in here, and I open each of them so I can decide which one is best. One is orange like a bad suntan, and I think Mom should throw it out immediately. Another is pink like a baby blanket, and I hate pink. The third is purple, like a really dark periwinkle, and I am about to put it on my lips, but I decide to open the fourth tube first.

And in the last tube is a brand-new, never-before-used, beautiful cherry-red lipstick. Slowly, I screw up the bottom of the tube, so that the lipstick slides out from the top in a perfect point, just like a rose growing out of the dirt. If this were my lipstick, I would use it every day, and I do not understand why Mom has not even worn it once yet. I wait until the lipstick is poking all the way out of the tube, then I lean very close to the mirror, place the smooth part from the top of the lipstick on my bottom lip, and spread. I do the same for my top lip, pressing my lips together like I see Mrs. Spangle do after she puts her lipstick on after lunch, and then pop them open again. I give my best Picture Day smile into the mirror, rub some lipstick off my teeth with my finger, and then clap my hands together once with excitement.

And I am fairly certain that I have never looked more beautiful in my life.

I place all the makeup back in the bag, and the bag back in the drawer, along with the lotion and Mom's hairbrush. Then I stick the tube of cherry-red lipstick in my pocket, grab the laundry

basket from the corner, and tiptoe out of Mom and Dad's bathroom.

And I do not even mind too much that I still have to clean up all of Timmy's toys, because I have found it: the perfect new accessory—one that Dennis cannot steal, because he can't scrape it off my lips, and one that Natalie cannot copy, because she is much too boring to wear lipstick.

And I think I am going to be the best-looking one in our class photo this year, because nobody else will be wearing cherry-red lipstick on Picture Day.

CHAPTER 6

Sharper Shoes

WHEN I CARRY THE LAUNDRY BASKET full of Timmy's toys downstairs and toward the toy room, Mom does not even say, *Thank you for cleaning up Timmy's mess, Mandy.* Instead, she says, "What did you do to your face?"

She yells it, actually. Loudly. So loudly that it makes a twin start crying, which serves her right, if you ask me. But before I can even answer, Mom continues, "Are you wearing my makeup?"

"Yes," I answer honestly.

"Why do you have my makeup on your face?"

"I had to practice," I explain.

"Practice for what?"

"Picture Day," I answer.

"You are not wearing makeup for Picture Day," Mom says. "You are in second grade. This isn't Halloween."

"I'm not going to wear *all* of the makeup," I say. "Just the lipstick."

"Oh no, you are not," Mom says. "Eight-year-olds do not wear lipstick."

"But why?"

"Because you're too young."

"I'm not a baby."

"I didn't say you were a baby, I said you were too young."

"But I like it."

"Just because you like it doesn't mean that it's appropriate, let alone for Picture Day."

"It makes me happy," I say in my sweetest voice, but Mom still looks annoyed at me.

"That still doesn't mean it's appropriate," Mom says. "You can wear lipstick when you're older."

"How old?"

"Eighteen," she answers, and my eyes grow as wide as pancakes then, and I drop the laundry basket on the floor with a crash.

I do the math quickly in my head. "That is in ten years. That is way too long."

"Maybe sixteen," Mom says. "But definitely not eight. Now go clean yourself up."

"Please?" I drag out the *e* in "please" so that it sounds like its own word. "Pretty, pretty please?"

"You know, Mandy," Mom begins, lifting the wailing twin onto her hip, "I was thinking about taking you along to run some errands at the mall tomorrow—just you and me—"

"For Picture Day?" I am suddenly very

excited. "To get me a new accessory?"

"No, to buy you and Timmy new shoes. Your feet are growing faster than your shoes can keep up with them. But I thought you'd like to come along and pick out your own pair."

"Yes!" I answer. "Yes, I would like to go and pick out my own pair. Pretty, pretty, pretty please with whipped cream on top?"

"I don't know," Mom shakes her head. "With you being so uncooperative these past couple of days, I think I'm going to have to change my mind and bring Timmy—"

"No!" I interrupt her. "I will stop being ornery. I would like to go to the mall. Please." I scoop the toys that have fallen out of the basket back inside as fast as I can, just to show Mom how cooperative I'm being.

"That's a good word—ornery," Mom says. "How do you know that?"

"Mrs. Spangle taught it to me," I say, but I do not tell her the part where Mrs. Spangle *called* me ornery, because I know Mom will ask what I was doing, and that is not something I would like to explain.

"And what are you going to do about your face?" Mom asks.

"Wash the makeup off," I say. "I will do it in a lick and a split. I promise."

"That's more like it," Mom says. "Keep being this cooperative, and we have a mall date for tomorrow."

"I will," I tell her, because not many things are worth cleaning up Timmy's toys and scrubbing cherry-red lipstick off of my mouth, but going to the mall with Mom is certainly one of them.

When I wake up the next morning, I stretch toward my toes slowly until I remember: It is Saturday, which means it is mall day, which means I get to choose my own pair of new shoes. And this is much better than having Mom choose new shoes for me, because she tries to make me wear shoes with laces, and I hate to tie laces.

"Wahoo!" I call out to myself, and I jump out of bed faster than I have ever jumped. I turn my bedroom doorknob so that the door flies open, and I pad down the stairs quickly.

"I am ready!" I announce as soon as I get to the kitchen, even though I am still in my night-gown and even though Dad is the only one there.

"Ready for what?" he asks before taking a sip of his coffee.

"Mom is taking me to the mall," I explain. "You are not allowed to come. You have to babysit Timmy and the twins."

"Sounds like fun. I think we'll all go," Dad says with a smile.

"No! Mom promised. Only me. No twins." I

say the last two words like there is an exclamation point after each of them. "And no Timmy. You can come, I guess, if you want to leave them home alone."

"I was just teasing you, but thanks for the half-hearted invitation," Dad says. "I don't think you're going today, though—Mom said she wanted to clean out the garage."

"What?! But I can't wait a whole other day," I tell him.

Dad shrugs. "You can take it up with your mother," he says. "Doesn't matter to me."

"*Mooooooommmmmm,*" I yell, dragging her name out so that it is many, many syllables, and then I remember that I am still supposed to be acting cooperatively, and I don't think Mom will think shouting is being "well behaved." "Where is she?" I ask Dad.

"In the twins' room," Dad says. "And try to

keep your voice down—Timmy is still sleeping."

I run to the twins' room and open the door slowly. Mom has both of them propped up on the changing table, and they are wiggling like octopuses.

"Oh, good," Mom says when she sees me. "Help me keep a hand on them, will you? They're wiggle worms today."

"No, thank you," I answer, because I try to never, ever touch the twins, especially when they are smelly and damp on the changing table. "When are we going to the mall?"

"After you help me with the twins, like I asked you to," Mom says.

"So today?"

"Yes, today," Mom says. "Now get over here. Keep a good grip on Cody while I change Samantha—careful, he'll try to get away from you."

I hold the twin down by his thighs, but he

tries to reach out and pull my hair, so then I hold his hands down, too. "Knock it off, twin," I say.

"Mandy, his name is Cody," Mom says. "How would you feel if he called you only 'Girl'?"

"I would not care," I say, because the twins do not even talk yet, so it is a silly question. "What time are we leaving for the mall?"

"After you change Cody's diaper for me," Mom says, grinning at me out of the corner of her mouth.

"That will never happen," I tell her.

"Well, it was worth a shot," she says, fastening the sticky tape on the other twin's diaper. "Here, carry Samantha to your father, and once you're all dressed, we'll get going."

I grab the twin around her waist like a sack of laundry and haul her to the kitchen.

"Here." I dump her on Dad's lap. Then I jog

up the stairs and change out of my nightgown as fast as I can.

And even though I want to, I do not take the cherry-red lipstick out from under my mattress and smear it on my lips, because I am very good at being cooperative today.

Mom holds my hand as we walk through the mall toward Small-Fry Shoes, and I skip next to her, because I am happy we are out together with no strollers and no diaper bags and no Timmy and no twins.

I also skip because Mom is walking very, very fast and my legs are much shorter than hers.

"Here we are," Mom says as we walk into the shoe store. "Go see what you like, but remember, only one pair." I let go of her hand to examine the thousands and millions of beautiful shoes on the shelves. I run my hand over a pair of sneakers with tie-dyed laces, and I pick up a blue shoe with glittery fireworks spreading across the toes. But then I see them: the most perfect, wonderful pair of shoes I have ever seen in my whole life. I lift one of them very carefully, using only the tips of my fingers so I do not leave any smudges, and I examine every inch of it.

The shoes are pale lavender, just like the crayon that sits next to the periwinkle one in my box of 152 colors. And they have flowers decorating the toes—flowers that stick out in every direction, which is much better than just having flowers painted on. Plus, some of these flowers are periwinkle, which is the best color in the whole universe.

But the flowers are not even the best part of this pair of shoes; the best part is that they have a heel—a real heel that would click-clack on the ground. And I have always wanted a pair of click-clack heels.

I carry the shoe over to Mom, who is looking at dinosaur sneakers for Timmy in the boys' section.

"Look," I say to her.

Mom glances over at me. "Pretty," she begins, "but impractical. We're looking for shoes you can wear every day. Do you think Timmy would like these dinosaur ones?"

"I will wear these every day," I tell her. "I promise. Every single day. Did you see the flowers? Some of them are periwinkle and everything."

"I said they're very pretty, but they're not the kind of shoes we're looking for today."

"But you said I could pick my own pair," I remind her. "And these are exactly the kind of shoes *I'm* looking for. I can even wear them on Picture Day."

"No one will be able to see your shoes in the school picture," Mom points out.

"But I will know I am wearing them," I reply, "which is the whole point of good shoes anyway."

Mom grins at me then, just a little bit. "You have a point," she tells me. "Well, there's no harm in you trying them on, right? But if they don't fit or they're uncomfortable, we're choosing another pair."

"They will be perfect!" I assure her, and I bounce up and down on my tippy toes because I am so excited to get these shoes on my feet.

Mom approaches the salesgirl who is leaning against the cash register. "Can my daughter try on these shoes, please?"

"Sure," the girl says, and she has a string of earrings flowing all the way up her ears. At the very top of each ear is a small flower, and it almost matches the flowers on my perfect shoes.

"Slide your foot in here," the girl says to me, and she takes off my shoe and pushes my heel all the way back against the edge of the size machine, which is cold against the bottom of my foot. "Size two," she announces, moving the metal bar on the machine to the tip of my longest toe. "I'll be right back." She picks up the sample shoe and walks with it into the room at the back of the store.

"Just so you know, Mandy," Mom begins, "if you really want to get these shoes once you try them on, that's it. No other new shoes and nothing else for your Picture Day outfit. You'll wear your periwinkle dress from the Presidential Pageant. Understood?"

"Yes." I nod my head ferociously. "These shoes are worth it."

"Well, see how you like them once they're on your feet," Mom says. "If they hurt, we're not getting them." The salesgirl with the whole ear of earrings comes back then, and she straps the shoes onto my feet. I stand up and take one step, and I hear the heel click-clack against the floor. My face spreads into an enormous grin, and I prance around the store happily.

"I will take these," I say to Mom.

"So that's it," Mom confirms. "No other shoes."

"Right," I answer.

"And you'll wear your periwinkle dress on Picture Day? With no complaints?"

"Yes," I agree. "No complaints."

"Are you sure?" Mom asks. "How about this adorable pair?" She points to a plaid shoe that does not even have a heel on the bottom. "I think they're really sharp."

"These are sharper," I say, pointing to my feet, and then I throw my arms around Mom's waist so that she knows that I mean it.

"All right, then," Mom says.

"Wahoo!" I call out, pumping my fist in the air. "Thank you! These are the best shoes ever!"

"We'll take them," Mom tells the earring girl, who smiles at me like we are sharing a secret.

"A girl always needs a good pair of fancy shoes, huh?" she says to me.

"Fancy-dancy ones," I agree. "They're even better than my sunglasses."

CHAPTER 7

Glittery Disaster

I SPEND ALL DAY ON SUNDAY TRAIPSING around my house in my new shoes. Dad says I need to stop clumping my heels so loudly against the tile floor in the kitchen, but I like the way they sound, so I do not listen. And Mom says I need to go outside and scrape the bottom of the shoes against the sidewalk so they are not so slippery, but I don't want to give them even one scratch, so I do not listen.

Then Grandmom comes over and says to

me, "My, those are just about the most beautiful shoes I have ever seen," and this is why I love Grandmom.

Plus, Grandmom likes to give me presents, and I love presents. So I am very happy when she starts digging in her handbag with a smile on her face.

"It's not new, I found it in my room," Grandmom tells me. "Just goes to show that you can find some wonderful items in your own closet." She pulls out a scarf that glitters and shimmers and shines in the light.

"Thank you!" I take the scarf from Grandmom and reach up so I can hug her tightly around the neck. "This is the best scarf ever."

"Not bad for a leftover, huh?" Grandmom asks.

"No, because it is not a leftover to me," I explain. "It is new." I run my fingers up and down the scarf and practice wrapping it around my neck, and then around my hair, and then around my wrist. I love it so much that I do not know what to keep my eyes on more: the scarf or the shoes. So I wrap the scarf around my ankles so that I can see both at the same time.

"Mandy, you're going to fall down. Untie that," Dad instructs me. "We don't need any more broken toes around here."

"But I like to look at both of them at the same time," I explain.

"I'm so glad you like your new accessory," Grandmom tells me. "But how about, if you want to look at your shoes and scarf together, you sit down to do so?" And I think this is not the greatest idea, because then I cannot make click-clack sounds with my heels, but I do not argue with Grandmom because she just gave me this glittery scarf, so she is pretty much my most favorite person in the world right now.

"I am wearing my new scarf to school tomorrow," I announce from the couch. "And my new shoes, too."

"I thought you wanted to save those shoes for Picture Day," Mom says, "so you can show them off with your matching periwinkle dress."

I consider this for one second. "Okay," I say. "But I am bringing the scarf."

And I just know that this scarf is too special for Natalie to ever figure out how to copycat it.

On Monday, I wear my scarf around my neck all the way to school, and everyone on the bus oohs and aahs over it, which I like a lot. When I get off the bus, I skip over with excited feet to my class's line in the gym, and I search the crowd for Anya's wispy blond curls.

"Anya!" I yell when I spot her. "ANYA!" Anya turns around.

"I LOVE YOUR SCARF," she yells back instantly.

"Me too," I say. "Do you think this is an outdoor accessory?"

"Hmm." Anya considers. "No, I think you can probably wear it in the classroom. Mrs. Spangle sometimes wears scarves inside."

"Good." I nod with satisfaction. "That's what I thought too."

"Ugly scarf, Polka Dot." Dennis appears behind me. "It matches your face."

"Quiet, Dennis," Anya says, defending me. "No one's talking to you."

"Yeah, quiet, Freckle Face," I agree. "My scarf is beautiful."

"Nah," Dennis says, and he reaches out to touch it, even though I never gave him permission to touch my things. "Eww, and it's scratchy, too."

"QUIET, Dennis," I yell louder, and I unwind the scarf from around my neck. "I hope it scratches your nose." I grab my scarf by the end and whip it toward Dennis's face, then I pull it back real fast so he cannot try to grab it.

"Excuse me," I hear from over my shoulder, and Anya gasps. And Anya gasping is never a good sign, I've learned.

I turn slowly and see my scarf—my beautiful, glittery, wonderful scarf—covering someone's face. And not just anyone's face: a grown-up's face.

The grown-up reaches his hand up to pull the scarf off of him, and that's when I see the person I have hit in the head: Principal Jacks.

Oh no.

"Mandy, right?" Principal Jacks asks me, but I am only able to stare back at him, my eyes so wide that they cannot even blink. I pull my scarf back into my own hands quickly.

"Yep, that's her name!" Dennis calls out when I do not answer. "Mandy Berr."

Without another word, Principal Jacks reaches out his right hand toward me, and for a second I think that he wants to shake hands, so I reach my own right hand out to do so. But Principal Jacks does not crack one smile.

"The scarf, please," he says. "This is going to live in my office for a while, until you learn not to use it like a weapon." I feel myself letting Principal Jacks take my scarf away, and even though I want to shout about it, or cry about it, or scream about it, my mouth is dry like cotton balls, and I say nothing.

And then I hear Dennis snort with laughter.

"Dennis Riley," Principal Jacks scolds him. "I have a feeling you weren't innocent in whatever the problem was here, so watch it. Remember what we discussed." Dennis's mouth falls into a serious straight line.

"Come to my office at the end of the week for your scarf, Mandy," Principal Jacks says to me. "And I hope you and I don't have to see any more of each other before then."

"Are you okay?" Anya asks me as Principal Jacks walks away, my glittery scarf trailing out of his hand and onto the ground.

"No." I shake my head. "I am not."

"What happened?" Natalie appears next to us, and she is just about the last person I feel like talking to right now. That is, except for Dennis.

"Mr. Jacks took away Mandy's new scarf because she hit him in the head with it," Anya explains, and I give her a dirty look about this. "I mean, it was an accident. It was all Dennis's fault."

"Was not," Dennis pipes up. "I'm not the one who brought the ugly scarf to school."

"You touched it," I remind him. "You are not allowed to touch my things."

Dennis shrugs. "You snooze, you lose, Polka Dot," and he walks to the back of our classroom line, because Dennis always likes to be the caboose.

I see Mrs. Spangle come into the gym then with the rest of the second-grade teachers, so I stand in line between Anya and Natalie. Natalie whispers in my ear, "I'm sorry about your scarf. Dennis is terrible." And I just nod my head sadly because that is the truth.

"Happy Monday!" Mrs. Spangle calls down our line. "Let's all scoot in and make our line the straightest in all of second grade. One head in back of the other." And I stare at the back of Anya's hair, my lips drooping lower and lower down my face into a frown.

Mrs. Spangle begins to walk down our line as the other second-grade classes file out of the gym. She stops when she gets to me.

"Why are you looking like such a sourpuss today, Mandy?" she asks. "It's Picture Day week, remember? Time for us all to practice our smiles. And I know how excited you are about Mr. Jacks's lunchtime contest."

I try to smile at Mrs. Spangle, because I do not want to tell her about my problem with the scarf or about getting in trouble with Principal Jacks, or else she might not like me anymore. And Principal Jacks not liking me anymore is bad enough.

Also, there is absolutely, positively no way that I would ever want to have lunch with the principal now, because thinking about him taking my scarf away makes my face feel hot and embarrassed, so the contest is not even fun anymore. I wish I could rewind my day to yesterday, when I had my click-clack heels on my feet and my glittery scarf around my neck, and the whole week was not already a big disaster.

CHAPTER 8

How to Say "I'm Sorry"

"HI, MANDY," MOM GREETS ME in the kitchen after school. "I'm surprised you're not wearing that scarf you love so much."

I nod my head slowly, because I do not really feel like talking about it. When I don't answer, Mom looks at me like she is suspicious. "Did something happen to your scarf?" she asks, and I almost wish that the twins were awake so that Mom would not be paying such good attention to me.

"It is a long story," I reply. "I will have it back at the end of the week."

"But where is it now?"

"I told you, it is a long story," I repeat.

"Well, I would like to hear this story."

I sigh a big gust of breath then and look toward the twins' room, hoping that one of them will begin wailing immediately. When that doesn't happen, I say, "It is missing right now."

"What do you mean, it's missing?"

"I do not have it."

"Did you lose it?"

"No."

"Did someone take it?"

"Yes."

"Who?"

I pause and think about how to answer this. "Principal Jacks," I finally confess.

Mom narrows her eyes at me. "Why did Mr. Jacks take your scarf?"

"Because I hit him in the head with it," I say. "But it was an accident—I was trying to hit Dennis."

Mom mumbles words under her breath that I do not think I am supposed to hear. "You hit your principal in the head? Mandy, for goodness' sake, what are we going to do with—"

"It was *Dennis's* fault," I say. "He was touching my scarf, and he is not allowed to touch my things."

"No matter." Mom waves her hand in front of her face, like she is batting away my comment. "I mean, Dennis should not be touching your things, yes, but when he does, you should tell a teacher about it. You need to stop trying to handle everything yourself. You're only making things worse."

And I do not say anything then, because I know that Mom is a little bit right.

"Maybe I'll write a note to Mrs. Spangle, apologizing for letting you go to school with all of those things," Mom says.

"Accessories," I correct her.

"What?"

"They are not things, they are accessories," I explain. "*Things* are boring; *accessories* are amazing." It is a very important difference, and Mom needs to understand it.

"Whatever they are, they're not working out too well for you, are they?" Mom says. "Should I write Mrs. Spangle a note?"

"No. She doesn't know about the scarf."

"Where was she when you hit Mr. Jacks in the head?"

"It was before school in the gym," I explain. "She did not see."

"Then you are going to write an apology note directly to Mr. Jacks," Mom tells me. "I should have thought of that in the first place."

"No, thank you," I answer, and I am polite and everything.

"I'm not asking, I'm telling, Amanda," Mom says, and she uses my A name, so I know she means business. "There's stationery in the junk drawer. Get to work."

I yank open the junk drawer and pull out piles of chip clips and rubber bands and magnets before I find Mom's seashell stationery, which is not even good stationery to have. If I had my own stationery, I would make sure Rainbow Sparkle was on it. Or at least some periwinkle polka dots.

I take a red pen out of the drawer too, even though I am not usually allowed to write with pen. (I wrote with purple pen on my seatwork the first day of second grade, until Mrs. Spangle made it a rule that we could not write with pens in the classroom. She put it on the rule chart and everything. It is not one of my favorites.) I shove twin stuff off to the side of the kitchen table and sit down to write.

Dear Principal Jacks, I begin. *I am sorry you took my glittery scarf. From, Mandy Berr.*

"I'm done!" I yell to Mom. "I need an envelope."

"Let me see that first," Mom says. She lifts up my note, takes a fast glance at it, and then rips it in two pieces. "Absolutely not," she says. "Try again."

"Why? I said I was sorry."

"You said you were sorry for something that happened to *you*," Mom explains. "Good apologies work only if you say you're sorry for what you did to someone else."

"I do not know what you're talking about."

"You said that you are sorry that Mr. Jacks took your scarf," Mom says.

"Right, that is what I'm sorry about."

"That is not an apology," Mom says. "An apology would be, 'I'm sorry I hit you in the head with my scarf.' Understood?"

"Ughhhh," I groan, and get up to grab another sheet of stationery out of the junk drawer.

Dear Principal Jacks, I write again. *I am sorry I hit you in the head with my scarf.*

"You can't write just one sentence, by the way," Mom calls from across the kitchen, as if she is reading over my shoulder. "You need to be more sincere than that."

It was not my fault, though, because Dennis was trying to touch it. Dennis Riley. You know him because he is always in trouble. From, Mandy Berr.

"Done!"

Mom comes over and takes the paper from my hand. Before I can stop her, the paper is in four pieces.

"I don't understand why you're making this so difficult," Mom says. "Here, I'll sit with you until you get it right. Grab another sheet of stationery."

I give Mom my "You are driving me bananas" face, but I do like that she is sitting with me, with no Timmy and no twins, so I do not argue about it.

"What are you going to write first?" she asks.

"Dear Principal Jacks, I am sorry I hit you in the head with my scarf," I say.

"Sounds good," Mom says. "Write." I do so, as neatly as possible because Mom is watching, and then I look back up at her.

"What can you write next?" she asks. "Remember, you want to sound sincere."

"What's 'sincere'?"

"Like you mean it," Mom says. "So what can you say?"

"It was an accident," I begin.

"Okay, then what?"

"But I should not have been throwing my scarf at Dennis," I finish. "Even though he was trying to touch it."

"How about just 'It was an accident, but I should not have been throwing my scarf'?" Mom asks.

"Fine," I say, and I write that sentence down. I do not make any mistakes either, so it doesn't matter that I'm writing in pen and cannot erase it.

"Good," Mom says. "How can you end it?"

"From, Mandy Berr."

"Not yet," Mom says. "You need a closing sentence."

"Hmm." I think. "How about 'I will try not to do it again'?"

"Excellent," Mom answers. "Only no 'try.' Write 'I will not do it again.' Because you will not, right?"

"I will try."

"Mandy," Mom says with a warning in her voice.

"Fine, I will not," I say, and I write out the sentence. "Can I end with 'From, Mandy' now?"

"Yep," Mom answers. "Then reread your work and make sure you haven't made any mistakes. I'll get you an envelope."

I finish my note, read the whole thing all over again, and then write Principal Jacks's name on the envelope. I fold the letter three times until it fits inside, and then I run my tongue over the sealer.

"Am I done now?"

"You're finished," Mom says. "Go stick that in your book bag so you don't forget it tomorrow. And make sure you bring it to Mr. Jacks's office first thing."

"I will," I promise. "Can I go to my room?"

"Okay. In thirty minutes, though, we're going to get started on homework," Mom tells me.

"Unless you want to get it over with before the twins wake up?"

"No, I need a break," I tell Mom very seriously, and this makes her smile a little in the corners of her mouth.

"Okay, thirty minutes," she tells me, and I scoot into the living room and place my note in my homework folder. "Hey," I call back over my shoulder. "Do you know how to snap?"

"Snap what?" Mom calls.

"Your fingers," I answer, walking back into the kitchen just as Timmy appears from the toy room. And before I know what is happening, Timmy lifts up his right hand, pinches his fingers together, and makes a huge, loud, enormous snap.

"I do," he says, and I feel my eyes grow as wide as pancakes. "Daddy taught me."

"How come Dad never taught *me* how to snap?" I ask Mom.

"I'm sure he'd be happy to show you," Mom answers. "And if he doesn't, I will. Or how about . . ." She raises her eyebrows then like she has a great idea. "Timmy can teach you."

"No, thank you," I answer. I cannot have a preschooler teaching me how to snap—that would just be humiliating. But Timmy has already grabbed my hand and is pushing my fingers together.

"This," he says, pointing to my thumb. "And this," he continues, pointing to my middle finger. He puts his own thumb and middle finger together, and—pow!—he snaps. "You do it."

I place my middle finger on my thumb, and I rub them back and forth against each other. Nothing.

"Fast," Timmy instructs.

I try again, and my middle finger just slides into my palm with no sound at all.

"Fast!" Timmy repeats, and he snaps again, which only makes me mad.

"You are not a good snapping teacher," I tell him, and I turn around and march toward the stairs. When I get to my room, I dig under my pillow for my bag of gummy bears, and then I reach far under my mattress until I find Mom's lipstick. I walk over to the mirror hanging on my closet door, untwist the lipstick tube, and spread the lipstick onto my lips. I will have to remember to take it off before Mom sees me, but I like wearing it now, just for me.

I bounce onto my bed and stick a gummy bear inside my mouth. Because I think gummy bears are the only ones besides me in the whole world who do not know how to snap.

CHAPTER 9

Snaptastic

I ARRIVE AT SCHOOL THE NEXT MORNING with my insides
feeling fluttery.

I am afraid to bring my apology note to Prin-
cipal Jacks, because what if he is still mad at me?
It is very bad to have the principal mad at you,
I think, so I have a jumpy feeling in my stom-
ach. If I could, I would never go near Principal
Jacks's office again, which is a shame, because
usually, I really like to be assigned the Class
Messenger from our chart of classroom jobs. I

like bringing the attendance sheet to the office and the lunch order to the cafeteria, because those are very important tasks. But from now on, when Mrs. Spangle tells me it is my turn to be Class Messenger for the week, I am going to say, *No, thank you.*

"Psst, Anya," I whisper when we are putting our book bags away in the cubbies. "Can you do me a favor?"

"What is it?" she asks.

"I need you to bring this note to Principal Jacks's office," I tell her. "Please."

"Why me?"

"Because you're my best friend," I say.

"Yes, I know," Anya says. "But why don't you want to go yourself? You love to go to the office."

"Not anymore." I shake my head back and forth sadly. "Principal Jacks doesn't like me because of the scarf thing."

"Okay," Anya says, and she reaches out and takes the note from me. "What should I tell Mrs. Spangle?"

"Tell her you have to drop a note off in the office," I say. "From your mom."

"My mom writes in cursive." Anya points to the name on the envelope. "And she would write 'Mr. Jacks,' not 'Principal Jacks.'"

"Don't show Mrs. Spangle the envelope," I say. "Just tell her you have to drop it off."

Anya walks over to Mrs. Spangle's desk, and I watch her hold up the blank side of the envelope. Mrs. Spangle nods her head, and Anya turns and winks at me.

She heads toward the classroom door, where she waves me over to meet her. I tiptoe to the door quickly.

"What should I say when I get to the office?" she asks.

"Tell Mrs. Gradey you have a note for Principal Jacks."

"Got it." Anya walks out the classroom door. "I'm on it!" she calls over her shoulder.

"Thank you!" I whisper-yell back, making sure that Mrs. Spangle cannot hear me.

"What're you two doing?" Dennis appears behind me.

"Mind your own beeswax," I tell him.

"You're not even going to call me 'Freckle Face' first?" Dennis calls after me as I walk to my desk.

"Leave her alone, Dennis," a voice says from behind me, and I turn to see what Anya is doing back from the office so soon.

Only the voice is not coming from Anya at all—it is coming from Natalie! Natalie is defending me, which is usually only Anya's job.

And even Dennis seems pretty shocked by

this, because he clamps his mouth shut immediately and does not say one more word.

"Hey, thanks," I say to Natalie when we are back at our desks.

"No problem," Natalie says. "Dennis is terrible."

"He really is," I agree, and I sit down at my desk and think for a moment about the note Mom made me send to Principal Jacks. Maybe, since Natalie is sticking up for me now, I should apologize to her, too, just this once. I turn to face her. "I'm sorry I was mean about your sunglasses. I really like them."

"Thank you," Natalie says. "I really like yours, too. That's why I got mine. Because they looked so nice on you."

"That's because fancy-dancy sunglasses make everyone look like a movie star," I tell her.

Our classroom door opens then, and Anya walks through with no envelope in her hands. She nods her head at me silently, and I nod back. And this is why it is very useful to have your favorite person in the world be in the same class: because she will understand when she needs to drop off letters to the principal's office for you.

But when that person is missing, it's not a bad idea to have a backup favorite person, too, I guess. Someone who will defend you to the most terrible person in the class.

Someone like Natalie.

The next morning I am feeling jumpy again, but this time it is more because I am excited than nervous. I am excited because it is PICTURE DAY, and I love Picture Day.

Plus, I have my new shoes to wear, and I cannot wait to show them off.

"Mom," I call down the steps as soon as I open my bedroom door. "I need help."

"With what?" Mom calls back.

"My Picture Day outfit."

I hear Mom climbing the steps. "You need me to help you get dressed? You usually hate when I try to help you."

"This is not a normal outfit," I explain. "I cannot get the periwinkle wrinkled." And I like the way "periwinkle wrinkled" sounds, so I say it again. Three times in a row.

"Okay, that's enough of that," Mom says with a smile. "Let's see what we've got here." She opens my closet and lifts the perfect periwinkle dress from the Presidential Pageant off of the pole. It is still covered in plastic from the dry cleaner, and I like that it has been kept so pretty. Mom breaks the plastic and pulls the dress out, and it is just as fabulous as I remember.

"Nightgown off," she says to me, so I strip down to my underwear and lift my arms over my head, waiting. Mom rolls the dress up and is about to drape it over my head when I stop her.

"Wait!" My arms fly down to my sides, and I skip over to my dresser. "I need my lucky underwear." I pull my favorite polka-dot pair out of the drawer and change into them, and Mom seems to think this is funny.

"You're really going all out for Picture Day, aren't you?" she asks.

"It is a very important day," I explain, and Mom pulls the dress all the way over my head, straightens out the shoulders, zips me up and buttons me in, and then ties the ribbon in the back for me. I reach under my bed and take out the shoe box with my new shoes, and Mom helps me place them on my feet, like I am Cinderella. Then she runs a brush all the way through my hair, until it falls into waves down my back, just like the ocean.

"All set!" Mom calls when she is finished. "You look pretty perfect to me." I click-clack over to my mirror and examine myself.

"Almost," I decide. "But I need a few more things first."

"Wahhh," a twin starts crying from downstairs, and I roll my eyes way up to the ceiling, because the twins really know how to ruin a good time.

"Come downstairs when you're done," Mom tells me. "I want to take a few Picture Day photos of my own." When Mom is gone, I retrieve my fancy-dancy sunglasses off of the shelf above my bed, and I stick them inside my pink handbag. I look over my shoulder to make sure no one is snooping, and then I reach under my mattress and take out Mom's cherry-red lipstick. I stick the lipstick in my bag too, and then I bounce down the stairs and click-clack into the kitchen.

And when Mom takes my first photo of the

day, I place my hands on my hips, stick my right foot out to show off my shoe, and smile like I mean it, because I do.

"Mandy, Mr. Jacks would like to see you" is the first thing I hear when I walk into my classroom, and it makes my day go from wonderful to terrible immediately.

"Oooh . . . ," Dennis says in a singsong voice. "Polka Dot's in trouble."

"Dennis, that's a warning," Mrs. Spangle scolds him. Dennis's Mohawk is combed down into a poof against the top of his head, and he is wearing a bow tie and everything. If "Freckle Face" weren't already such a great namecall for him, I'd come up with a new one right away, because he looks pretty silly right now.

I scurry up to Mrs. Spangle's desk so that we can talk in private.

"Why does Principal Jacks need to see me?" I whisper.

"I'm not sure," she says. "There was just a note in my mailbox this morning asking to send you down to his office when you arrived." Mrs. Spangle raises her eyebrows at me. "Did something happen that I should know about?"

I swallow loudly. "Well, there was this scarf . . . ," I begin.

"Uh-huh . . ."

"And I kind of accidentally hit him with it, but it was an accident, I promise, because I was trying to hit Dennis, and then Principal Jacks took my scarf away, and I wasn't going to tell you because I didn't want *you* to be mad at me too, but I sent him a note and I said I was sorry and—"

"Okay, okay," Mrs. Spangle interrupts me. "Best to just go see what he wants. And, Mandy?

I don't want you to be afraid to tell me things. I'm here to help you."

"Okay," I say quietly, and I turn on my click-clack heel and head out the classroom door, walking as slowly as possible in the direction of the office.

The second I arrive at the window by Mrs. Gradey's desk, she calls out to me. "Oh, Mandy Berr! Mr. Jacks is expecting you," she says. "You can head right in."

I shuffle my feet on the floor in the direction of Principal Jacks's office. "My, don't you look all dolled up and lovely for Picture Day today," Mrs. Gradey calls after me. But I am too fluttery about where I am headed to do anything but give her the very smallest of smiles.

"Mandy Berr!" Principal Jacks's voice booms out even before I reach his doorway. "Just the second grader I wanted to see. Come on in."

I walk in carefully, and my knees feel like I can hardly bend them. I've never been called to the principal's office before—never because the principal asked to see me. That only happens to really bad kids. I'm more of a get-my-initials-on-the-board-a-couple-times-a-week type of kid. But never this.

"Well, you look spiffy today," Principal Jacks says when he sees me. "Is that a special outfit for Picture Day?"

I nod my head silently, and I am pretty sure I have never been so quiet in my life.

"I wanted to thank you for the note you sent me," Principal Jacks continues. "That was very nice of you to apologize. It takes a big person to admit when she's made a mistake."

I nod my head again, because I do not usually like to admit such things.

"And I wanted to give this back to you."

Principal Jacks reaches into his desk drawer and pulls out my glittery scarf. "I assume you know not to throw it in anyone's face anymore, correct?"

"Correct," I answer. "Thank you very much, Principal Jacks."

Principal Jacks smiles at me then, and his owl eyes crinkle on the sides. "Are you going to wear the scarf for Picture Day? It sure is nice."

"I think I will," I answer him. "Along with some other accessories."

"Sounds like a plan," Principal Jacks says. "Make sure you smile widely."

"I will," I answer him. "Can I ask you something?"

"Of course."

"Can you teach me how to snap?" I ask. "You know, your fingers. Like you did in Mrs. Spangle's room. Everyone knows how to snap but me, and I have always wanted to know how."

"Absolutely," Principal Jacks answers. "I've taught many kids to snap over the years, and you look like you're coordinated enough. Are you?"

I nod my head up and down quickly.

"Okay, then," Principal Jacks continues. "Which hand do you write with? That will be the easier hand to learn on."

I lift my right hand in the air. "I know I use my thumb and my middle finger," I tell him. "But I can't get them to make the sound."

"That's because no one taught you the trick," Principal Jacks says. "The trick is that when you place your middle finger on your thumb, you have to place the whole top part—not just the fingertip by the nail. Let me see." I hold out my right hand to show him. "Perfect. And instead of placing your middle finger square on the top part of your thumb, you need to slide it a millimeter or two higher. Almost like it is touching your thumbnail." Principal Jacks holds out his hand to show me, and I copy what he is doing.

"Then, when you're ready and your fingers are squeezed just tightly enough together—like Goldilocks, not too hard and not too soft—you bring your middle finger

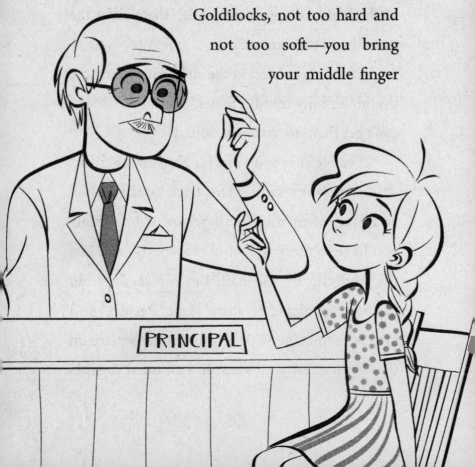

down toward your palm as quickly as you can and—" *Pow!* He snaps. "You try."

I raise my right hand in the air, place my middle finger on my thumb, and then pull it to the top so that it is almost touching the nail. I take a big breath, concentrate very hard, make a little wish, and then—

Pow!

"I DID IT!" I call out to Principal Jacks, and if he weren't sitting behind his desk right now, I swear I would throw my arms around his neck. "You are the best snapping teacher ever!"

"Nice job, Mandy Berr," Principal Jacks says. "Now, remember, snapping is only for special snappy occasions, so you need to keep it under wraps when you're in school, or else you may wear your fingers out."

"I will," I say. "And I will smile widely in my Picture Day photo too. I promise."

"Good," Principal Jacks says. "Now you better skedaddle back to Mrs. Spangle before she thinks you got lost."

So I turn around and trot out of Principal Jacks's office, click-clacking on the floor with my glittery scarf around my neck, and I am pretty sure I have never smiled more widely in my life.

CHAPTER 10

Principal Pals

PICTURE DAY IS PRETTY MUCH THE LONGEST day ever, because Mrs. Spangle's class does not get to have our photos taken until the very last hour of the day. I think this is bad scheduling, because I would like to go first. Plus, now I have to keep my Picture Day outfit perfect all day, including during recess, and that is a very long time to be neat.

Finally, Mrs. Spangle says that it is time. As the rest of my class scurries into line, I dart over to my cubby and pull my pink handbag off of the top shelf. Then, at the last moment, I take my glittery scarf, too, and I walk on my tiptoes to the end of the line. Anya leaves her own place in line to come stand next to me.

"Are you wearing all of that stuff in the picture?" she asks me.

"They're accessories, and I don't know yet," I answer. "Can you hold this for a second?" I hand her my scarf and dig into my handbag for Mom's lipstick. I wish I had remembered to find a small mirror to stick in my bag too, so I could see as I put it on my lips, but I have practiced enough times by now that I should be good at it.

I swipe the lipstick across my bottom lip— one way and then the other—and then I move to my top lip, being careful to create a mountain on each side, with a dip in the middle.

"How does it look?" I ask Anya.

"Excellent," Anya says. "Do you want me to put your scarf on you?"

"Yes, please," I say, and Anya drapes the scarf over my neck. I place my handbag on my shoulder and stare at my fancy-dancy sunglasses for a moment.

"I shouldn't put the sunglasses on my head, right?" I ask.

"Nah, that would be too much," Anya replies. "You're good like this." Anya is wearing new cowgirl boots with gemstones running up the sides, and I like them a lot, because they also have heels that click-clack on the ground while we walk.

My class's line weaves its way through the hallways and into the cafeteria, where all of the camera equipment has been set up on the stage.

"Welcome," the photographer greets us, and he is wearing a scarf around his neck that is the color of many butterflies. And I would kind of like to wear it myself, if I am being honest.

"We're going to start with your class shot," he tells us. "Follow your teacher up to the stage, and we'll assemble you according to height."

I raise my hand, and when Mrs. Spangle spots me, I gesture for her to come over.

"Yes, Mandy?" she asks when she reaches me.

"I would like my shoes to show in the picture," I whisper to her. "They're the best part of my outfit."

"Are you wearing lipstick?"

"Yes?" I answer like it is a question because I am not sure why Mrs. Spangle is asking.

"Does your mom know you have lipstick on for the picture?"

"No," I reply honestly. "But it's her lipstick, so she should not mind."

"Are you sure?"

I nod my head up and down, even though I

am not positive that Mom will not mind. But it is *my* picture, so I think I should get to wear lipstick if I want to.

"Okay, then," Mrs. Spangle says.

"Now, about my shoes . . ."

"You have to sit where the photographer tells you," Mrs. Spangle says. "You'll look pretty no matter what, don't worry." She pats me on the shoulder.

"You there in the purple." The photographer points at me. "Let's have you sit on this chair here on the end."

"It's periwinkle," I tell him.

"Even better," he says. "Right there on the end." He points to the row of chairs, which the tallest kids in my class are all standing behind. I sit there obediently and glance at Mrs. Spangle, who nods her head at me.

"You with the bow tie"—he points to Dennis—"right there next to Miss Periwinkle."

"Her name is Polka Dot," Dennis says, and he shuffles his feet over to the chair next to me and plops down. He plops down so hard that the chair scrapes against the floor and out of the line.

"Dennis," Mrs. Spangle says with a warning in her voice, "fix that chair, please. And, Mandy, put your purse underneath you. You don't need it for the picture."

I raise my hand and gesture for Mrs. Spangle to walk over to me again. I wiggle my finger until she leans down close to my face, and then I whisper in her ear, "Do I have to sit next to Dennis?"

"Yes," Mrs. Spangle answers, and it is in her "I mean business" voice, so I do not argue with her.

"Try not to break the camera, Polka Dot," Dennis whispers to me, and I notice then that part of my dress is caught between our chairs. I pull it out carefully.

"Don't wrinkle my periwinkle, Freckle Face," I tell him.

"Wrinkle my periwinkle," he repeats. "That sounds funny."

"I know," I say. "I like it too."

The photographer assembles the rest of our class in three rows—some standing, some sitting in chairs, and some sitting cross-legged on the floor. He leads Mrs. Spangle to the back row next to the standers, and she is posing right behind my head, so I look up and grin at her. Then I cross my feet at my ankles, just like the photographer asks, and stick them out as far as I can, my toes pointed, so that my shoes will be in the picture.

"What a fine-looking group of second graders," a voice booms out from the cafeteria door, and Principal Jacks appears. "Thank you for being so patient today—I know it's hard to be the last group."

"Okay, on the count of three," the photographer begins, "say 'Fluffernutter!' One . . . two . . ."

"FLUFFERNUTTER!" my class calls out, and the photographer snaps the picture with a click.

"One more," he announces, "and then we'll move on to your individual shots. One . . . two . . ."

"FLUFFERNUTTER!" we call again, and I smile my widest smile, because I am in my periwinkle dress and my click-clack shoes and my glittery scarf and, best of all, my cherry-red lipstick. So it does not even matter that I am sitting next to Dennis, because I have a lot going on.

"Looks great, guys," the photographer says.

"If I could just interrupt you for one second," Principal Jacks states, coming onto the stage. "I want to announce the results of our raffle drawing, because the first contest winner is from Mrs. Spangle's class. This person will have lunch with me this Friday and will also get to choose

one buddy to accompany her to the lunch."

"Her?" Dennis calls out. "So it's a girl?" He says the word "girl" like it is a disease, and I hope he gets in trouble for it.

"It is indeed, Mr. Riley," Principal Jacks answers him. "And I hope you are happy for your winning classmate and remember what we discussed." He gives Dennis a very serious look with his owl eyes. "Where is Natalie Abel?"

Natalie, who is sitting cross-legged on the floor, raises her hand shyly.

"Congratulations, Natalie!" Principal Jacks exclaims. "You displayed excellent cafeteria behavior all week. As a reward, you get to choose one buddy to join you for lunch, so think about who you would like that to—"

"I choose Mandy," Natalie interrupts him, and I have never been so shocked in my life.

"Very good." Principal Jacks nods. "I look forward to dining with you. Now go take some stupendous pictures." He turns and walks out the cafeteria door while Natalie looks over her shoulder at me. I give her an enormous smile and a thumbs-up, and Natalie mouths, *I like your lipstick.*

Thank you, I mouth back with no sound, and Natalie grins at me.

"Okay, let's get you all lined up for your individual shots," the photographer announces. "Let's start with Miss Periwinkle here on the end." He points to me.

"Wahoo!" I leap up from my seat and reach down to grab my handbag. Then I take off running in the direction of the giant blue screen with the camera set out in front of it.

"Mandy, no run—"

SPLAT!

Suddenly, my hands and knees feel cold against the floor, and my scarf falls completely over my head so it is covering my hair like a blan-ket. I lift my chin and see my handbag lying far out in front of me.

"Mandy, are you okay?" I hear voices behind me, and I feel someone tap my arm and try to help me up. I turn around expecting to see Anya or Mrs. Spangle or even Natalie, but instead, I come face-to-face with a splattering of freckles. Dennis's freckles.

"You all right, Polka Dot?" Dennis whispers to me. I raise myself onto my knees, and Dennis boosts me up by the elbow.

"Why are you helping me?" I ask.

Dennis shrugs. "It was either that or step on you," which is a very Dennis way to answer.

"Well, thanks," I say, and Mrs. Spangle appears over my shoulder. "Are you okay? What happened? You know you're not supposed to run indoors."

"I just got excited," I answer. "And I slipped in my new shoes." This is probably why Mom kept telling me to go scrape the bottoms on the sidewalk outside—so they would not be so slippery.

"I think you should go get checked out by the nurse," Mrs. Spangle says. "You fell pretty hard."

"But my picture!" I exclaim. "I need my picture taken first."

"Fine," Mrs. Spangle answers. "Picture first—Dennis, you too—then Dennis will escort you to the nurse."

I look at Dennis, but he only nods very seriously, and I am not sure what has gotten into him.

I walk over to the blue screen—slowly this time—and climb onto the stool. I drop my handbag by my feet, right by my perfect shoes, and I smile my widest grin toward the camera. The photographer adjusts my glittery scarf, and the light flashes in my eyes.

"All set," he says, and I wait for Dennis to be finished with his own picture before we begin walking to the nurse's office.

"Why are you being so nice to me?" I ask. "What do you want?"

"Can't I just be nice once in a while?"

"You are usually not," I say.

Dennis laughs at this. "Principal Jacks said I had to start treating people like I want to be treated, so . . ." Dennis trails off.

"Is that why he keeps saying to remember what you talked about with him?" I ask. "Is that what he said when you stole my gummy bears?"

Dennis nods his head without speaking.

"So you want me to be nice to you?"

"Only sometimes, I guess," Dennis answers. "Or else it's no fun."

I think about this for a moment. It *would* be pretty boring if I had to be nice to Dennis all the time.

"Here is a deal," I begin. "We don't have to be that nice to each other. Just if it's like an emergency or something."

"So I still get to call you 'Polka Dot'?" Dennis asks. "After all, you do call me 'Freckle Face,' so I'd say we're even."

"Okay, fine," I answer. "How many Band-Aids do you think the nurse will give me?"

"Try to get a whole box full," Dennis answers, and I nod because that sounds like a good plan. "By the way, why did Natalie pick you to go to lunch with her?"

"Because I'm fun," I answer him, and this comment makes Dennis laugh again.

"I guess you are, Polka Dot," he says.

* * *

Mom comes to pick me up at school, even though I am not really hurt. The nurse called our house to say that I fell down, and because Grandmom was already there, Mom could leave her with Timmy and the twins and come get me by herself. Which is a great thing, except for one small detail. . . .

"Are you okay?" Mom asks when she barges into the nurse's office. "What hurts? Did you scrape anything? Let me see your—*are you wearing lipstick?*"

Uh-oh.

"Yes," I answer honestly.

"Did you wear that in your picture?"

"Yes."

"Mandy!" Mom wails, and she doesn't even seem worried anymore that I fell down. "You can't wear red lipstick in your class photos! What will the other parents think?"

"They'll think she looks nice," Dennis pipes up from the cot behind me.

"That's Dennis," I say, introducing Mom to him. "We only hate each other sometimes now."

"Hi, Dennis," Mom greets him before turning back to me. "So let me guess: You wore the scarf, too?"

"Yes," I say.

"I thought Mr. Jacks took it."

"He did, but he gave it back."

"Why?"

"Because he liked my apology note."

"Did you wear your sunglasses, too? Please tell me you didn't wear your sunglasses."

"You ask a lot of questions," Dennis chimes in again, and I laugh at him because I agree. "You sound just like my mother."

Mom ignores him. "Mandy, your school picture is supposed to be *nice*," she complains. "Wearing red lipstick, let alone all of that other nonsense, is not appropriate."

"It's cherry-red lipstick," I correct her. "It says so on the tube."

"Where did you even get that lipstick? Did Grandmom give it to you? Because if she did, I really have to have a talk with—"

"I took it," I say, "from your bathroom drawer."

Mom sighs enormously then. "Let's go." She motions for me to stand. "We'll finish this discussion at home." She leads me out of the nurse's office, thanking the nurse along the way, and back toward Mrs. Spangle's classroom. Dennis trails behind us.

"Mandy Berr!" Principal Jacks greets me in the hallway. "Are you all recovered?"

I nod my head. "This is my mom."

"Nice to meet you, Mrs. Berr." Principal Jacks shakes her hand. "That's quite the daughter you have there."

"Oh, she's something all right," Mom says. "I hope you know how sorry I am about the scarf—"

"Make no mention of it. Mandy and I got it all straightened out, didn't we?" He turns to me.

"Yep," I answer, and I raise my right hand in the air, press my thumb and middle finger together just like Goldilocks—not too hard and not too soft—and *pow!* I snap.

Principal Jacks snaps back at me with a wink. "Maybe you could teach Mr. Riley here the trick I showed you." He turns to Dennis and pats him on his combed-down Mohawk. "Unless, of course, you already know how to snap."

Dennis shakes his head back and forth, and he looks pretty sad about it, actually.

"I will show him," I promise Principal Jacks. "And you remember that Natalie is taking me as her guest when she has lunch with you?"

"I do. I look forward to seeing you both there," Principal Jacks answers.

"That's very kind of Natalie," Mom says. "Well,

it was nice to meet you," she adds, turning to Principal Jacks.

"Likewise," he answers. "That's some bold lipstick you're wearing, Mandy. It looks like you've eaten an entire bowl of cherries." And I smile super wide at Principal Jacks then, because that is exactly what I want to look like.

"Yeah, sorry about that," Mom says to him. "It won't happen again."

"A little lipstick never hurt anybody," Principal Jacks tells her. "See you later, Mr. Riley." He pats Dennis's head again as he departs, and Dennis scurries ahead of Mom and me into our classroom.

"See?" I say to Mom. "Principal Jacks likes my lipstick."

"Principal Jacks is not your mother," she answers. "Hand it over."

"Please, no," I beg. "Can't I keep it? If I promise to never, ever be ornery again?"

"That's a pretty big promise for you." She sighs again. "We'll talk about it later. Go grab your book bag." She points me toward my classroom.

I walk inside carefully, being sure not to slip again, and I go right over to Natalie's desk.

"Can you do me a favor?" I whisper in her ear, digging in my handbag as I do so. "I need you to play hide-and-seek with this." I hand her the lipstick tube.

"Huh?"

"I need you to hide this for me."

"Why?"

"My mom wants to take it away, but if I do not have it anymore, she can't," I explain. "So can you keep it for me?"

"Sure," Natalie answers. "No problem."

"If you want, you can wear some yourself," I offer. "I do not have any sick germs."

"You won't care that I'm copying you?"

I think about this for a moment, and then I shake my head. "Nah, we can both wear the lipstick. And our fancy-dancy sunglasses. We can be twins. But not twins like the twins at my house, because they are awful."

This makes Natalie's face break into a big smile. "We can wear them for our lunch with Mr. Jacks," she suggests.

"Perfect," I agree. "And I like to call him 'Principal Jacks.' Because he is the principal."

"Principal Jacks," Natalie repeats. "Got it."

"Thank you for picking me for the lunch," I tell her. "That was really nice of you."

"You're welcome," Natalie replies. "I didn't really want to win the contest at all. I'm a little afraid of Principal Jacks."

"He is not so scary," I say. "I promise. And plus"—I point to the tube in Natalie's hand—"we will have our cherry-red lipstick to protect us." I take the lipstick back for one minute and spread some across my lips, and then I return it to Natalie. I walk over to the cubbies and get my book bag before returning to the hallway to meet Mom.

"Lipstick?" Mom asks, reaching out her hand.

"I don't have it anymore," I tell her.

"Mandy," Mom says in her warning voice. "Don't lie to me."

"I'm not lying!" I promise. "I don't have it anymore—Natalie does."

"Why?"

"Because she liked it," I answer. "And you said I should be flattered when someone likes what I'm wearing, remember? So I gave it to her."

"That was pretty nice of you," Mom says. "Only, it was *my* lipstick, remember?"

"But you never even wore it," I remind her. "And red lipstick should always be worn by somebody, because it is beautiful."

Mom smiles at me a little bit then. "Next time just ask me first. I may have given you the tube to use for Halloween. You're right, I don't really like red lipstick."

"Well, that's perfect, because I love it," I say. "You can give me all of your red lipsticks from now on." I grab Mom's hand, and we walk out the front door of the school together. I click-clack my heels against the sidewalk and feel my glittery scarf blow in the breeze.

"Just a second." I drop Mom's hand and reach into my pink handbag, and I pull out my fancy-dancy sunglasses and stick them on my nose. "Okay, ready." I take Mom's hand again and squeeze it tightly as we walk to the parking lot.

Because sometimes, having Mom all to myself is my favorite accessory of all.

Mandy's Lessons:

1. NEVER TRUST A COPYCAT.

2. BE VERY CAREFUL WITH BOYS AND HANDBAGS.

3. CONTESTS ARE ONLY FUN WHEN YOU WIN THEM.

4. YOU CANNOT PLAY HIDE-AND-SEEK IF NO ONE IS
   LOOKING FOR YOU.

5. THE BEST WAY TO CLEAN UP A MESS IS TO MOVE IT TO
   ANOTHER ROOM.

6. A NEW OUTFIT IS GOOD, BUT A NEW PAIR OF SHOES IS
   BETTER.

7. DON'T HIT YOUR PRINCIPAL IN THE HEAD, EVEN BY ACCIDENT.

8. IT IS HARD TO WRITE AN APOLOGY NOTE IF YOU ARE
   NOT SORRY.

9. BEING SENT TO THE PRINCIPAL'S OFFICE IS NOT ALWAYS
   A TRAGEDY.

10. NEVER WEAR RED LIPSTICK ON PICTURE DAY.

DON'T MISS MANDY'S NEXT ADVENTURE,

Pizza is the Best Breakfast
(AND OTHER LESSONS I'VE LEARNED)!

IT IS NOT MY FAULT THAT there is chocolate pudding in Timmy's hair.

Mom says that it *is* my fault, of course. She thinks that just because I pulled the pudding cup away from Timmy, and it squirted on his face when I squeezed it, that this whole chocolate pudding thing is my problem.

But I promise that it is not.

"You said I cannot eat pudding for breakfast," I tell Mom, still holding the almost-empty pudding cup in my hand. She lifts Timmy onto the counter to sit and begins running a wet paper towel down his bangs.

"You can't," Mom answers.

"But Timmy was," I point out. "And that is not allowed."

"You're right, that's not allowed," Mom says. "But you had no business grabbing the cup away from him like that. You should've just told me."

"Then you would have called me a tattletale," I tell her, which I think is a pretty good point.

Mom sighs an enormous gust of breath—so enormous that the tippy-top of Timmy's hair blows a little from her nose wind.

"Timmy should not have been eating pudding for breakfast—do you hear that, Timmy?" Mom lifts his chin up to face her, and he nods, even though he is still licking chocolate from his lips. "But, Mandy, you did not have to intervene.

Next time—and there better not be a next time, Timmy—just come get me."

"So I should tattletale."

"Mandy," Mom says with a warning in her voice. "Enough."

When Mom's back is turned, I stick my longest finger inside the pudding cup and swoop up the last bite. Then I drop the cup onto the counter, because I am not cleaning up a three-year-old's trash. No way!

"Mandy eat pudding," I hear Timmy call then, and I whirl around on my heel to face him. He is pointing at me as Mom wrings his hair into wet tangles. "Mandy eat pudding too. I saw."

"Worry about yourself, Timmy," Mom says. "And, Mandy, throw that pudding cup away for me, please." I pick the cup back up and stomp toward the trash can, and I wiggle my finger through the pudding one more time, just to swipe up the last of it, before I toss it in the garbage.

"You're welcome, Timmy," I call, and he does not even say thank you for throwing out his trash, which I think is rude. I am pretty sure that if Timmy had to throw out my trash after I ate pudding for breakfast, I would have had to say thank you, so I stick my tongue out at him.

"Okay, I think it's all out now," Mom says, and she grunts as she hoists Timmy off the counter. But I think she should have left the pudding in his hair, because then at least the front of it would have been brown like mine. Not that I would like to look like Timmy, but I also do not like that he gets to have blond hair and I do not. At least the pudding would have made things even.

"You're going to be late for your bus, Mand," Mom says as she rinses her hands in the sink.

"Mandy," I correct her.

"I know your name, silly," Mom says. "Mand is just short for Mandy. It's affectionate."

"I do not like it," I tell her.

"I thought you didn't like Amanda."

"I do not like that, either," I say. "I like Mandy. With a *y*. The *y* is the best part."

"You have a lot of rules, you know that?" Mom says, and she kisses the top of my head. "Skedaddle. Your bus will be here in two minutes. Remember your jacket. And be careful of the twins on your way out, please."

I trot out of the kitchen and Timmy calls, "Bye, Mandy!" after me, but I do not answer him. The twins are lying on the living room carpet like blobs, looking at mobiles. I hold my nose as I step over them, because one of them always seems to stink like a dirty diaper.

I grab my book bag and open the front door before I remember.

"When is Paige coming?" I call to Mom.

"Tonight," she yells back.

"But what time?" Paige is my favorite cousin in the whole world, and I haven't seen her since last Christmas, which I think is way too long.

"After dinner. Grandmom is going to pick her up at Uncle Rich's house this afternoon," Mom tells me.

"And she is going to sleep in my room, right?" I ask. "Like a slumber party?"

"That's the plan," Mom answers.

"Wahoo!" I open the front door all the way and then slam it behind me, dragging my book bag along the ground as I gallop like a pony toward the bus stop.

Because if there is one thing that puts me in an excellent mood, it is Paige, because Paige is fabulous. That is her favorite word—"fabulous"— which is perfect because that is exactly what she is. Paige looks like a princess with very, very curly hair and real pierced ears, and her lips are so pink that she always looks like she is wearing lipstick, even though she is not. Plus, Paige does not have any brothers or sisters, which is what I would like to have, except that sometimes I like to pretend that Paige is my sister. She would be a much better sister to have than the twin, because even though Paige is already ten years old, she never cares that I am only eight. Because I am her favorite cousin too, just like she is mine.

And favorite cousins are absolutely the best kind to have visit you.

"Psst." I lean up against my desk and hiss at Dennis. *"Psst*, Freckle Face." I tap on the edge of his desk, which is now directly across from mine. He used to be in the row behind me, but Mrs. Spangle moved him next to me last week as a

way to make sure that we get along more than we argue with each other.

I do not think this plan is working so well.

"What?" Dennis runs his hand over the top of his Mohawk. We are supposed to be creating maps of our neighborhoods with construction paper, but Dennis doesn't seem to be doing much more than petting his own hair.

Actually, I have always wondered what the top of a Mohawk would feel like, if I am being honest.

"Are you done?" I point to his paper, which looks even worse than the artwork Timmy makes in preschool.

"Yeah."

"Can I use your glue stick?" I whisper. "Mine ran out." I screw up the bottom of the stick all the way so Dennis can see that it's empty.

"No."

"Why?"

"Because I said so, Polka Dot," Dennis says.

"But it's right there." I point to his glue stick, which is lying next to scraps of multicolored construction paper. "You didn't even put the cap on. It's going to dry up if you don't let me use it."

"Too bad for you," Dennis says, and he thumps his head on his desk and pretends to nap. I look toward Mrs. Spangle's desk, and she has her own head buried in her bottom drawer, digging through her handbag. I peer over the side of Dennis's desk until I can see his face, and he has his eyes closed, ignoring me.

So I reach very slowly behind his head, and I lift his glue stick with the very tips of my fingers. Careful not to create any breeze near his Mohawk, I pull my arm back as gently as possible. Success! I pump a silent fist in the air, still clutching Dennis's glue stick, and that's when I see Natalie staring at me.

I pull my other hand across my mouth and then stretch my lips tight, as if I had just zipped them closed, and Natalie nods to show that she understands she shouldn't say one thing. Natalie is almost like a real friend ever since she helped me hide Mom's red lipstick on Picture Day. Not like a *best* friend, like Anya is, but she is okay sometimes.

I use Dennis's glue stick to finish putting together my map, and I think about returning it to his desktop before he notices. But Dennis didn't even let me use his glue stick in the first place, so I don't think he deserves to have it back, at least not yet. I grab the cap from where it is resting just above his Mohawk, place it on the stick, and put it in my own desk. Then I place my empty stick behind Dennis's head.

"I like how nicely you've all been working on your maps," Mrs. Spangle says, standing up from her desk. "Anything you don't have completed can be wrapped up after recess—you'll all have five minutes to finish. Right now, though, let me see whose group is ready to line up for lunch."

I fold my hands neatly on my desk and sit up super-duper straight, just like Natalie always does. Dennis still has his head resting on his desk, and he is going to ruin it for our whole team. "*Psst,* Freckle Face." I try to kick him under our desks, but I can't reach. "Wake up."

"I am up," Dennis says, but he still does not lift his head, which means Mrs. Spangle is never going to call us to line up first. I stop sitting super-duper straight, since Dennis is wrecking it for our whole group anyway, and instead, I dig through my desk until I find my sticker book. Anya and I, and sometimes Natalie, have been collecting stickers and trading them, but mine are some of the prettiest, I think. My favorite kinds of stickers are filled with gel, and when you press them, the gel spreads out and looks glittery. I even traded most of my Rainbow Sparkle stickers for Anya's gel ones, because that is how much I love them.

"Mandy and Dennis, I'll wait," Mrs. Spangle says, so I place my sticker book on my lap and fold my hands again on top of my desk. Dennis places his chin on his hands but still doesn't lift his head.

"Sit up!" I whisper-yell at him, and he does, but not even super-duper straight like he is supposed to.

"Okay, Mandy's group," Mrs. Spangle finally announces. "You can grab your things from the cubbies and get in line." I stand and hold my sticker book up in Anya's direction to make sure she has hers too, and she nods at me. And then I scramble to grab my lunch box and get in line as quickly as I can so I won't be all the way in the back, because

Dennis always likes to be the caboose. And there is no way I want Dennis to ruin my appetite today.

"Why'd you steal Dennis's glue stick?" Natalie asks me when we reach our table in the cafeteria.

"I didn't steal it, I took it," I explain.

"Isn't that the same thing?"

I think about this for one second. "No, because if I stole it, I can never give it back, like when Dennis stole my gummy bears and ate them all. If I took it, I can give it back. I just don't want to yet."

Natalie nods like this makes sense, and I am a very good explainer, I think.

I whip my sticker book onto the table and open to the center page, which has all my favorite gel stickers in a row. "Aren't they beautiful?" I ask.

"They are," Natalie agrees. "My mom said she would take me to the teacher store and look for more stickers this weekend." Teacher stores are one of the best places for getting stickers, because teachers like to buy them almost as much as we do. I have never been to a teacher store, even though I have wanted to go to one my whole entire life. Mom says we do not have to go there because no one in our house is a teacher, but Mom doesn't understand important things like sticker collecting.

"I wonder if Paige has any stickers she would trade," I begin. "Did I tell you she is coming tonight?"

"Only like a thousand times," Anya answers. "I know, you're excited."

"Who's Paige?" Natalie asks.

"Her cousin," Anya answers for me. "Her *favorite* cousin." She drags out the word "favorite" as she says it and wiggles her head back and forth.

"Why is she your favorite?" Natalie asks.

"Because she is fabulous. That is Paige's favorite word, you know—'fabulous.' And that's what she is."